The Magical Pink Pendant

A Witch's Cove Mystery
Book 9

Vella Day

The Magical Pink Pendant
Copyright © 2021 by Vella Day
Print Edition
www.velladay.com
velladayauthor@gmail.com

Cover Art by Jaycee DeLorenzo
Edited by Rebecca Cartee and Carol Adcock-Bezzo

Published in the United States of America

Print book ISBN: 978-1-951430-26-9

Don't get me wrong. I love magic, just not when it is used for evil.

It's bad enough when some poor soul is murdered in my hometown, but when he's near and dear to someone I care about, I have no choice but to look for the killer. Since magic seems to be involved in his death, my teenage cousin and I might be the only ones who can discover the killer's identity. After all, we are witches.

I was hoping this would be a run-of-the mill case, but no. The number of suspects keeps mounting, making our job more difficult. Considering most suspects live across the state makes it doubly hard.

Can we say road trip!!

Seriously, this person is super dangerous, and we have to take precautions. But never fear, between my trusty talking pink iguana, my very talented business partner who has mad computer skills, and my teenaged psychic cousin, we're sure to crack the case.

Chapter One

THE SOUND OF hard pounding footsteps racing up the outside staircase of our Pink Iguana Sleuths' office, caused a rush of hope to surge through me. This could be a paying customer! While my business partner—turned boyfriend—and I were no longer desperate for funds, I needed something to keep me mentally engaged. As much as I liked my former job as a waitress, it didn't stimulate my math brain like solving a murder did.

Before I had time to even push back my chair from my computer desk, Gavin Sanchez, my cousin's new beau, slammed open the door. While the nineteen-year-old normally acted in control, right now, he looked scared and rather confused. The red-rimmed eyes were a definite cause for concern.

"Is Rihanna here?" His words gushed out, and my heart broke at his distress.

Before I could tell him Rihanna was in her room, she ran out and stopped dead in her tracks. "Gavin, what's wrong?" Her voice cracked.

"My father is…dead." He waved his arms, looking as if he punched the air hard enough, answers would miraculously appear.

His shocking statement had every cell in my body freezing. "What? He's dead? How?"

Rihanna had the sense to hug her boyfriend and then lead him over to the sofa. I was glad she didn't escort him into our converted storage room turned bedroom since nosy me wanted all of the details.

I know it might seem strange that my eighteen-year-old cousin, Rihanna Samuels, would be living at an office, but until she graduated from high school in a few months, she would be staying with us here—or longer if she so chose. Having her around made my life a bit more complete.

"I'll get you something to drink." The part of me that used to be a waitress often took over in a crisis.

Since Gavin frequently stopped over, I knew which soda he preferred. I also fixed a sweet tea for both me and Rihanna. Not wanting to miss even a word of this tragedy, I hurried.

Let me mention that I, Glinda Goodall, along with Jaxson Harrison, run a sleuth agency, because…well…being a busybody is in my nature—as is being a witch.

I carried the drinks into the main room, placed them on the coffee table, and then sat across from them. "When you're ready, tell me what happened."

Gavin sat up straighter, his gaze bouncing around the room. Clearly, he was in shock, as anyone would be upon learning his not-very-old dad was dead. Poor guy. Gavin was already living under the stress of interning with his medical examiner mother. Having to deal with the death of a parent would crush anyone.

When he finally seemed to get himself under control, he blew out a breath. "Okay. Here goes. Nash got a call earlier this morning about a body in the backyard of our neighbor's house. Since the victim—my dad—wasn't carrying his wallet or anything, Nash had no idea who this person was, which meant he had to run a fingerprint scan."

"That must have come as a shock to our deputy." I couldn't imagine how hard it would be to tell your girlfriend that her former husband was dead.

"Nash said he was upset, which was why he asked the sheriff to double-check his findings."

"That makes sense." Considering where his dad was found, the sleuth in me immediately suspected foul play. "Who's backyard?"

"Mrs. Prentiss'."

"She's in her eighties." I didn't believe she'd be capable of harming a man in his prime.

"She is. Here's the bizarre part. Dad had been renting a room from her for the last three days."

I couldn't help but suck in a breath at that news. First off, his Miami-based father was supposedly quite wealthy. I would have thought he'd have stayed in the Magic Wand Hotel, our nicest facility, rather than rent a room in someone's slightly rundown home.

"I take it you didn't know he was in town?" If Gavin or Elissa had been aware of his dad's visit, surely they would have suggested a better place—or maybe that would just be my reaction.

Gavin shook his head and then sipped his drink. "Neither of us had any idea he was here. When we'd Skyped, Dad never mentioned any plans to see me. The last time we chatted, all he could talk about was his upcoming trip to Rome with

Morgana."

The emphasis on that name implied she wasn't high on Gavin's list of favorite people.

"Morgana is his new wife, right?" He'd mentioned her before, but clearly, I hadn't paid enough attention.

"Yes."

"Did you talk to your dad often?" It was important to understand how close they were.

"He'd set up a time most weeks to connect via Skype, but too often something would come up, and he'd have to cancel." Gavin shrugged, pretending it was no big deal, but the disappointment slicing across his face said otherwise.

"Lawyers are busy people." I hoped that would make him feel better. Doctors were busy, too, but I bet his mom would never cancel on him like that—or at least not very often.

"So he kept telling me." Gavin pressed his lips together.

"Do you have any idea what business he had in Witch's Cove, or why he didn't tell you he was here?" Rihanna asked.

"No, and it's not like Dad not to mention something that important. I don't remember him keeping secrets from us."

While this might not be a paying job for Jaxson and me, for my cousin's sake, I had to do what I could to help.

"What did your stepmother say about his visit here?" Despite some tension between them, I hoped Gavin had spoken with her.

"Morgana was as surprised as we were. My dad told her that he was going to Tallahassee for some lawyer's convention." His voice trembled, but I couldn't tell if it was from anger, frustration, or sadness.

If Mr. Sanchez lied to his new wife and son, he was hiding

something. But what?

Before I could come up with a list of possibilities, the office door opened. When Jaxson came in and smiled at me, my tight muscles relaxed a bit. His presence and level-headedness always helped calm me.

He stopped short when he spotted Gavin. Jaxson looked back at me and then at the young couple. "What happened?"

The fact Gavin and Rihanna were on the sofa talking to me probably clued him in that things were amiss. They usually preferred their privacy. "Grab a chair, and we'll fill you in."

He'd just sat down when Iggy, my fifteen-year-old pink iguana familiar popped in through the cat door.

"I'm getting too old to be climbing that railing," he complained. "You need to put in an elevator for me." For effect, he expanded and contracted his tiny chest. I'm guessing it was to show us he was out of breath, but I knew a faker when I saw one.

The idea of an elevator for a nine-pound iguana was ridiculous, but knowing Jaxson, he'd probably try to rig up something just to make Iggy happy.

I patted my thigh. "Iggy, come over here. There's been a death."

Acting as if he hadn't just climbed a mountain, Iggy raced over. "Who died? Do we get the case?" he asked with too much enthusiasm.

I was thankful that Gavin couldn't hear him—only witches and those who'd had a spell put on them, like Jaxson, could. However, Rihanna had explained to Gavin that the rest of us could communicate with my ego-driven, talking lizard.

"Gavin's father," I whispered. I lifted him up onto my lap and pressed a finger to his mouth. Iggy could say some insensitive things at times, which wasn't cool. Gavin might not be able to hear, but Rihanna could.

"Is he asking about my dad?" Gavin nodded to my familiar.

"Yes." I didn't think translating what Iggy said would be helpful. "Rihanna, how about bringing Jaxson and Iggy up to speed?"

She outlined the series of events—or at least as much as she knew.

"How did he die?" Jaxson asked.

"I don't know," Gavin said. "It wasn't anything obvious like a gunshot wound or a blow to the head. Mom called in another medical examiner from Ocean View to do the autopsy."

That was a good idea. She wouldn't want any impropriety. The law might believe she'd tamper with the evidence—being his ex and all.

"From Mom's brief perusal of the body, it was sometime around two this morning. The medical examiner will know more after he finishes with the autopsy."

I wanted to ask where his mother was at the time of Gavin's father's death, but it wasn't my place. If confronted, she'd say she was home in bed, which was probably true.

"Did your mom say if he'd been ill?" I asked. "His death could be from natural causes."

"No. As far as we know, Dad was healthy."

"Does your mom think someone murdered him then?"

"It's not her place to guess, but Nash thinks so, only he

isn't telling me why," Gavin said.

This must be terribly traumatic for Gavin. I had to say, the young man was holding up rather well. I'd be bawling my eyes out if anything happened to either of my parents.

At least Rihanna would be able to relate to Gavin since her father had been murdered five months ago.

"What can we do to help, Gavin?" Jaxson asked.

"Nothing. I didn't come here for that. I just needed to see Rihanna and tell her what happened."

I could understand that. "Rihanna, why don't you take Gavin into your room where you'll have more privacy."

She nodded. As soon as they slipped into the bedroom and closed the door, I faced Jaxson. "I can't even imagine what Gavin is going through right now, but we need to do something."

"We'll help in any way we can just as soon as we learn that Mr. Sanchez was murdered."

I picked up my tea and sipped it, my mind racing. "Why would Daniel Sanchez rent a room down the street from his ex-wife and son and then not contact them?"

"Maybe he was spying on them."

"Spying? Why?"

"I don't know. Perhaps he heard that Elissa was seeing someone, and Daniel wanted to make sure this man wouldn't be a bad influence on his son," Jaxson said.

"That makes sense, but I would think Gavin would have given him the lowdown on Nash since Gavin and his dad were in regular contact. If Daniel didn't want to talk directly to his ex-wife about Nash, why not have Gavin meet him for dinner in town or somewhere else to discuss it?"

"Those are excellent questions," he said.

"I understand wanting to check out Nash, but staying a few doors down the street is almost asking to be spotted."

"For sure."

"Forgetting why Daniel Sanchez was in town or the reason for staying so close to his ex-wife, why would someone want him dead? I don't recall hearing that he'd been to Witch's Cove in a long time even though his parents live here."

Jaxson huffed. "I have no idea, but didn't you tell me he'd recently remarried?"

"Yes."

"Maybe the new wife thought he wanted to get back with his ex-wife and ordered a hit on him. Trouble in paradise is often a good motive for murder."

I held up a finger at his wild imagination. Having crazy hypotheses were usually up my alley. "Mrs. Sanchez claimed she didn't know he was here."

"People lie."

"True. It's possible either Daniel came to Witch's Cove to make amends with Elissa, or because their divorce had been so contentious that he wanted to clear the air in order to get a fresh start with his new wife. When he spotted Elissa cozying up to our deputy, Daniel might have decided to sit back and watch before making his move."

"Could very well be. That might explain why he didn't meet up with his son. Maybe he didn't want Gavin to tip off Elissa that he was in town," Jaxson suggested.

"Too bad all of these theories are pure conjecture. But you know who might have the deets on what really happened between our good medical examiner and her former husband?"

"Pearl?"

"Precisely." Pearl Dillsmith was the sheriff department's receptionist. She kept the job in her old age mostly because her grandson was now the sheriff. "If Pearl is privy to what could have happened, her best buddy Dolly would have gotten the lowdown by now, too."

Jaxson rubbed his stomach. "I'm so hungry."

He was mocking me. "You can just say we need to go to the diner in order to talk to Dolly. There's no need for the hunger ruse. You know I'm always up for eating."

Jaxson chuckled, as I'd hoped.

Iggy looked up at me. "Can I come?"

"You know it's hard to talk to you without looking like I'm crazy, and when I don't speak to you, you can get huffy."

"Me? Huffy? I'm a model citizen."

"Sure, you are." I cleared my throat. "I think you'd be better off spying on the two teens."

He lifted his chest. "Spy? Me? I never would do that."

"I wasn't born yesterday." His favorite pastime was listening to conversations—especially private ones.

Iggy dropped onto his stomach. "Fine. What's your best bet on the motive for killing this guy? Greed, revenge, or jealousy?"

"Let's not jump to any conclusions. We don't know that he didn't die from natural causes."

"But suppose he was killed?" Iggy asked.

"Fine. I'd go with jealousy." I honestly had no idea, but Iggy would keep bugging me unless I picked an option.

Iggy bounced up and down. "That sounds juicy."

I wagged a finger at him. "Juicy, maybe, but not substantiated. We probably should rule out revenge, though." I was only kidding. I never eliminated any motive until I had proof—at least most of the time.

"Why?" Jaxson asked, clearly not understanding I wasn't serious. "Gavin's dad was a lawyer. Perhaps one of his clients was convicted due to Sanchez's poor handling of the man's case. If he'd recently completed his sentence, he'd be free to come after him."

I sunk back against the chair. "According to Gavin, his dad won most of his cases, implying he was a good lawyer. In case he did mess up, this opens up a whole slew of suspects."

"The sad part is that we can't eliminate anyone who is still in jail. When I served time for my bogus crime, too often I'd hear stories about an inmate hiring someone to exact revenge for him."

"That stinks. What's worse is that the suspects are probably still in Miami, which is a huge town." At least when a murder happened in Witch's Cove, it was moderately easy to keep track of their comings and goings. We had eyes and ears everywhere, mostly in the form of our gossip queens.

"How about we let Iggy do his magic with the teens, and you and I hit up the Spellbound Diner? You know Dolly will be on top of things, what with Pearl on the case," Jaxson said.

"I love a good plan." And something sweet to eat.

Chapter Two

BY THE TIME Jaxson and I walked into the Spellbound diner, it was close to four. The timing was quite good since the lunch crowd had left, and the dinner crowd had yet to arrive. I liked that if we bent Dolly's ear, we wouldn't be taking her away from any demanding customers.

Dolly spotted us right away and nodded. From her distressed look, she'd heard about the sad news. While Daniel Sanchez wasn't a member of the Witch's Cove community, his parents lived here, as did his former wife and son. It was an unspoken rule that we would do what we could for them.

Once seated, Dolly delivered two glasses of water. "I take it you heard what happened last night?" she asked.

"Yes. Gavin came over to be with Rihanna, but he wasn't able to tell us much. I think his mom might be trying to shield him from the horror." Dolly nodded. "Have you heard anything?"

"Just that his wife is on her way up here. I imagine she wants to see him—for closure and all."

"For sure." I sipped my water. "Did Pearl mention the cause of death or if they had any suspects?"

"Not yet, but Steve is driving down now to help coordinate things with the Miami PD."

"I'm surprised he'd take the trip before he learned if Daniel Sanchez had been murdered."

Dolly leaned in. "I know, right? Something hinky is going on. What was a man like Daniel Sanchez doing renting a room at Mimi Prentiss' house in the first place? I heard it's not the cleanest." She scrunched up her nose.

Gavin had been right. Something was off. "No speculation about who might be guilty then?" I asked.

A small smile came to Dolly's lips. "Not yet, but at great personal sacrifice, I put my sister-in-law on the case. If you think I like to gossip, that woman—Nora—is the worst. If she didn't live in Miami, and if she wasn't in Sanchez's social circle, I never would have asked her. She loves to hold it over my head that she is superior to me."

"I'm sorry. But it's fantastic that we have a connection to someone who might know what was going on in Daniel Sanchez's life before he came here."

A group of people piled into the diner. Really? I'd hoped it would remain empty.

"True." Dolly looked over her shoulder at the newcomers. "I guess I need to take care of them. What would you guys like?"

"I'll have a chocolate shake." I needed the comfort food.

"Coffee, black," Jaxson said.

Dolly smiled briefly and then went over to the new customers to seat them.

"Having an insider in Miami is good." I always tried to find the proverbial silver lining.

"It is. I think we can do some research even without Nora though."

"How?"

Jaxson leaned back in his seat. "Via Elissa Sanchez. At some point, she'll become frustrated with the pace of the investigation and ask for our help. I wouldn't be surprised if she has an idea who might have wanted to harm her ex-husband. Maybe not names, but whether it could be one of his co-workers or some disgruntled client. They must have talked periodically regarding Gavin's internship and such."

"True, but why ask for our help? Because we might care more about Daniel Sanchez—a man we've never met—than the sheriff?" I needed to answer my own question. "She'd never think that."

"She might not, but somehow we always manage to find the one clue that unlocks a series of events that leads Steve and Nash to catch the killer. I realize Nash would do everything in his power to solve this, in part because he cares for Dr. Sanchez, but what if magic is involved?"

"Magic?" I whispered. "I will admit that many of the deaths we've investigated had some element of it, but how would some lawyer from Miami have anything to do with that?" I leaned closer. "You don't think he could be a werewolf or a warlock, do you?"

"No, or rather not that I've heard mentioned."

I raised my brows. "I can't imagine Elissa Sanchez marrying him if he had been."

"Probably not, even though her current beau breaks that rule, right?"

"You have a point." So what if Nash Solano was a werewolf. Elissa Sanchez had come a long way since first arriving in our town. Learning about witchcraft and then werewolves had been difficult for the scientist. I was proud of her for being willing to bend her belief system and embrace new ideas.

A few minutes after Dolly seated this new group, she delivered our order, though I was no longer in the mood to indulge in the sugary delight. After seeing how angry, frustrated, and hurt Gavin had been, my heart kept breaking over and over again.

I pulled out my phone. "I'm sure my mom's heard about what happened, but I want to ask her to contact us if Elissa lets her know anything about the cause of death." I imagine the medical examiner doing the autopsy would keep her up-to-date on his findings.

My mom and dad ran the local mortuary, and as such, she and Elissa Sanchez had become friends, which served our agency very well.

"You're not even considering that he could have died of natural causes?" Jaxson asked.

I shrugged. "I could go either way. Lawyers are under a lot of stress, which could lead to all sort of physical ailments. On the other hand, lawyers often have enemies. We should have asked Gavin what kind of law his father practiced. We don't know if he even dealt with criminals. He could have been a civil lawyer."

Jaxson sipped his coffee. "No matter the law, there is always a winner and a loser."

"You're right. I'll text Rihanna since she'll still be with him." It was easier than doing a search on my phone. A moment later, she responded. "He's a divorce attorney."

"That almost guarantees someone will be upset with the outcome," Jaxson said.

That was true. "Do you think Gavin's dad mentioned anything about his purpose for being in Witch's Cove to his landlady, Mrs. Prentiss?"

"I don't see why he would, but there's one way to find out." He wiggled his eyebrows, clearly wanting to help lighten the mood.

My muscles relaxed knowing Jaxson was completely on board with solving the mystery of the man's death. "The preliminary report on the autopsy probably won't be finished until tomorrow if we're lucky, so for now, interviewing the last person to have seen him alive—other than the possible killer—is our best bet. I'm quite certain Nash has already picked her brain, but from what I recall, Mrs. Prentiss might need some prompting to remember all of the details."

"She's not reliable?"

I shrugged. "She's old, so I'll let you be the judge."

Once we paid, we hopped in Jaxson's car and drove to Dr. Sanchez's street. I'd delivered some funeral flowers to Mrs. Prentiss' house after her husband had died, so I knew where she lived.

"Fingers crossed her memory is working today," I said, mostly to myself.

At the front door I knocked, but it took her a minute to answer. "Yes?"

I tried not to let my disappointment show that she didn't recognize me. That was a shame since she and her husband used to eat at the Tiki Hut Grill quite often. "Mrs. Prentiss?"

"Yes."

"Hi, I'm Glinda Goodall, Fern Goodall's niece?" I hoped that she remembered my aunt, at least.

"Ah, yes. You delivered those pretty flowers after Sam died."

Okay, I was impressed that she remembered. It had been a few years since her husband had passed. "Yes. And this is my partner, Jaxson Harrison."

She ran her gaze up and down his body, confirming she wasn't dead yet. "How can I help you?"

"I was wondering if we could ask you a few questions about Daniel Sanchez."

Her cheer disappeared. "Of course. Such a tragedy. Come in."

The inside was dark and quite dingy, but all of the knick-knacks crammed onto the many shelves implied this was her comfort zone, and that was all that really mattered.

Jaxson and I sat on the sofa, while she sat across from us on a hard-backed chair. "I don't know how I can help. I already told that nice deputy everything I know." She looked to the side. "Though my memory isn't what it used to be."

I smiled. "That's okay. Did Mr. Sanchez tell you why he was in town?"

"To see his former wife, I believe."

I thought he would have come to visit his son, though Daniel Sanchez might not have wanted to tell Elissa's neighbor the truth. "I guess he saw her a lot then since she lives so close."

"I never saw them together, but Mr. Sanchez would leave around eleven in the morning and not return until about five in the afternoon. I figured he was visiting her at the morgue."

"Interesting." If Dr. Sanchez was to be believed, he hadn't visited her even once. So, what was he doing during that time?

Visiting his parents at their downtown bookstore? Or was he checking up on a client whose spouse lived in Witch's Cove? Ugh. We had too many options.

"Mrs. Prentiss," Jaxson said. "How did Mr. Sanchez seem to you?"

"Seem?"

"Did he appear happy, concerned, troubled, excited, or what?"

She huffed out a breath. Her brows pinched, and her eyes seemed to lose focus for a moment. "I'd say more troubled than anything."

"Why do you think that might have been?" Jaxson asked.

"I don't know. Just an old lady's spidey sense." She waved a hand. "It's not my place to pry into what is troubling a person. I just rent out the room."

That was nice of her to be so considerate. "Did he say how long he planned to stay?"

"No, but he paid for three days in advance when he first showed up. I didn't have anyone else booked for the remainder of the week, so I told him he could stay as long as he wished."

"He paid in cash, I take it?"

"Oh, my yes. I don't have any of those fancy computer things to help me with credit cards."

"I understand. One more question. On the night he died, why was he outside?" He could have gone into the backyard to have a smoke, I suppose.

"He offered to carry the garbage can in from the curb and put it in back. He was such a nice man."

"At two in the morning?" I had to assume the estimate for

the time of death was fairly accurate.

"I don't know the time. I'd gone to bed at around nine, and he said he would take care of it. When I knocked on his door the next morning to tell him I'd made breakfast, he didn't answer. I only looked outside to make sure the trashcan was where it was supposed to be. That's when I saw him and called the sheriff's department."

"How terrible for you to have found him like that." I looked over at Jaxson. "That's all the questions I have for now. Jaxson?"

"I'm good." He stood. "Thank you, Mrs. Prentiss. We appreciate you taking the time to help us."

"Anytime. Do you know how he died?" she asked.

"No. I wish we did."

"I hope it wasn't anything I gave him to eat. He might have been allergic to the peanut butter cookies I made."

"I'm sure he would have smelled the peanut butter and not eaten them." I hoped that was true.

"You might be right."

We left and headed back to the office. "Was that a total waste of time?" I asked.

"Who knows? Sometimes even the tiniest detail can prove useful later on," Jaxson said.

"Let's hope."

When we entered the office, I stopped short. A beautiful redhead was sitting across from Gavin and Rihanna. While I couldn't be positive, I figured this might be Morgana Sanchez, Daniel's second wife.

She turned around and dabbed her eyes. The woman stood. "I'm sorry to barge into your office, but my son said he was here."

Her son? I didn't get the sense that Gavin thought of her as a mother in any sense. I held out my hand. "I'm Glinda, Mrs. Sanchez, and this is Jaxson. I am so sorry for your loss."

"Thank you."

"Please sit down." A cup of coffee with peach lipstick on the rim sat on the coffee table in front of her. Good for Rihanna for being such a good hostess.

I probably should head on home, but I didn't want to miss the chance to pick her brain a little. Her sophisticated air gave off an odd vibe, but that might be because I was just a small-town girl.

To be thorough, I had to consider her a suspect. She could have realized she'd made a monumental mistake marrying him and felt she had to do him in.

Yes, I know I had to stop making up unfounded scenarios. A rampant imagination muddied the waters, which was never a good thing.

As Jaxson dragged over his office chair, I sat next to her. "Do you know why your husband was in Witch's Cove?" I asked.

"No. He told me he was going to a conference in Tallahassee. I had no idea he was here until your sheriff called and told me the terrible news."

At least her story was consistent with what she'd already told her stepson. "That must have come as a shock." I turned to Gavin. "Did the medical examiner figure out the cause of death yet?" I assumed his mother would call him the moment she learned anything.

"No. He still has tests to run."

I returned my focus to Morgana. "Did your husband have any medical issues?"

"His heart was giving him trouble."

"Dad was sick?" Gavin asked, a rush of concern coloring his tone. "He never said anything."

"He didn't want to worry you."

If anything, Gavin looked more upset than before. Poor kid. "By any chance, was your husband allergic to peanut butter?" I explained my reason for asking.

"No. He loved it."

Mrs. Prentiss' cookies had not been the cause of death then. I wanted to ask Mrs. Sanchez if she had any idea who might have wanted to harm her husband, but until we learned that Daniel Sanchez was murdered, there seemed to be no point in asking.

Not wanting to interfere with their time together, I stood. "I need to be heading on home, but feel free to stay as long as you need."

When I motioned with my eyes that I thought we should give them some space, Jaxson stood. "Me, too."

Iggy was somewhere about, but he'd either want to stay with Rihanna or head back when he could. If Mrs. Sanchez said anything interesting, Iggy would be the first to report it.

I was lucky to have such a sneaky little sleuth.

Chapter Three

A S SOON AS we left the office, I waited until we'd reached the bottom of the steps before getting Jaxson's opinion on Morgana Sanchez.

"She doesn't seem all that broken up about her new husband's death, despite the tears," he said.

"I agree, but maybe she is in shock. Morgana might not believe he's really gone until she sees the body tomorrow." I shuddered to think of the day I had to view a loved one that way.

"You might be right. Mind if I stop over?" Jaxson asked. "We should work on how to help Gavin."

I tossed him a brief smile. "I'd like nothing more."

No sooner had we stepped into my apartment when my cell rang. "It's Elissa Sanchez." My pulse skipped a beat. She rarely called me. Had she learned the cause of death already?

"Put her on speaker."

"Hey, Dr. Sanchez." I plopped down onto the sofa, and Jaxson slid next to me.

"Gavin told me you heard what happened to Daniel."

"Yes, my condolences." That platitude just slipped out. The two hadn't been together for a long time, and from what Rihanna had said, there hadn't been much love between them the last few years of their marriage.

"Thank you. I…ah…have a problem that I'm hoping you can help me with—or rather help Dr. Alvarez, our visiting medical examiner."

Jaxson's wide eyes crinkled his forehead.

I was surprised at her request. "What can I do?"

"Do you think you can come over to the morgue now?"

"Did something happen?"

"Not exactly, but Dr. Alvarez can't figure out Daniel's cause of death—at least not before the tox screens come back—but he said he's never seen anything like it before."

That was intriguing. "Sure. I'm with Jaxson. Is it okay if he comes?"

"Of course, and bring your necklace."

"My pink pendant?"

"Yes."

"We'll be right over." I was pretty sure Jaxson would agree to accompany me.

"Great. I'll be waiting for you."

I disconnected, and then Jaxson took my hand. "You don't look happy," he said.

"I'm good. It's just I'm usually the one to beg Dr. Sanchez to let me do my pendant test on the corpse. Now that she's asking me, I'm feeling the pressure."

Jaxson tugged her into his embrace. "You'll do great, but I thought she wasn't supposed to have anything to do with the autopsy—orp wasn't that her decision?"

"I don't know, but whoever it was, it was a smart one. I guess there is nothing illegal in having her watch."

"You're probably right. Let's go."

I always wore my pink pendant, so there was nothing to grab, other than my jacket, phone, and keys. Once downstairs, we jumped in his car. While the morgue was close, it was chilly out, and I wasn't in the mood to walk. Besides, Dr. Sanchez's request sounded urgent.

As soon as we reached our destination, Jaxson parked, and we rushed up to the front door where Dr. Sanchez was waiting for us. "Come in," she said.

Most of the lights in the main entrance were off, which seemed a bit strange, but I thought it best not to question her. When she led us into the autopsy room, I had to cover my nose, despite being rather accustomed to the smell of death.

"Where's the other medical examiner?" I asked.

"I waited until he went home before calling you. Technically, I shouldn't be with the body. I could be a suspect, and even if I weren't, asking a witch to use a magic pendant would be out of his comfort zone."

"I get it." Just a few months ago, she was a skeptic, but I wasn't about to bring that up either.

On the counter sat a container that she picked up and placed on the autopsy table. "I know you normally scan the whole body, but we've already narrowed Daniel's death down to there being an issue with his heart."

"His wife said he had heart problems."

Dr. Sanchez stilled. "You spoke with Morgana?"

"Briefly. When Jaxson and I were at the diner, Mrs. Sanchez showed up unexpectedly at the office where Gavin was visiting Rihanna. We only spoke briefly when we returned."

"How did Gavin act around her?"

She seemed to want my honest opinion. "I didn't get the sense he was overly pleased to see her."

"I imagine not. He and Morgana are like water and oil. I'm kind of hoping the tragedy will bring them closer. He'll need all of the support he can get."

"Rihanna will help."

"Yes, of course. She is wonderful, and Gavin thinks the world of her."

Jaxson nodded to the container. "Had you been aware that your ex had health issues?"

"No. Then again, Daniel and I haven't communicated in a few months. I'm not surprised he wasn't in perfect health since he was always under a lot of stress from having to deal with his parents, his new job promotion to full partner, and then getting married. It would put a toll on anyone."

"Are you saying his lifestyle could have been the cause of death?" Jaxson asked.

"Often yes, but not in this case. He died from heart failure for sure, but the other medical examiner believes he had help. He's testing for poison now, but I don't think he'll find anything." She held up a finger. "You said you were at the diner?"

"Yes."

The briefest of smiles crossed her face. "Did the gossip queen have anything to add about what might have happened? I know how connected she is to the pulse of this town."

Elissa knew how Dolly worked. "Sort of." I explained about Steve being on his way to Miami, but I bet Nash had already told her that much. "Dolly's sister-in-law lives in Miami and says she is on the case. Apparently, Nora knows a lot of the same people Daniel did."

"That makes me feel better. In the meantime, Glinda, I'm hoping you can perform your pendant magic."

I understood that she didn't want to prejudice me by further giving me more information. "I can try."

When Dr. Sanchez removed the container's lid, I sucked in a breath and covered my nose. "What is it?"

"It's the heart—or at least what is left of it. Since he was alive and seemingly well a few days ago, we can't account for it being so black and hard now. There is nothing that we know of that would do this." She lifted a hand. "I only saw this after Dr. Alvarez removed the organ. He asked my opinion because he'd never encountered anything like this before."

"I bet he hasn't." It was horrendous. I lifted my necklace out from under my pink turtleneck and unclasped it. "I've only done full body scans, but I don't see why I can't check out just the heart."

Not that I'd asked, but the good doctor and Jaxson moved back. Even though the object to be tested was small, I slowly swung the necklace across its base, the same as I would for the full corpse. Back and forth, back and forth. The pink stone immediately turned a bright yellow, and my heart spiked. Yellow meant magic. Was that what this was? A curse?

I didn't want to jump to any conclusions, so I continued. I also didn't look at Jaxson or Dr. Sanchez, but I was sure they were enthralled at such a blatant color change. When I finished, I turned to them. "I have a theory, but to be certain, I'd like to do my test on the whole body if you don't mind."

"Not at all, but I saw the stone turn yellow. Isn't that conclusive enough?"

"Yes, but perhaps something else will show up if I check the rest of the body."

"Of course. Good thinking."

Dr. Sanchez retrieved the corpse. I pretended he was some John Doe and not Gavin's dad. Once he was situated on the table, I started again, trying to ignore the findings about the heart. Even at the feet, the faintest yellow glow appeared. As I neared to where the heart had been, the stronger the color became. Once I finished with the head, I faced Dr. Sanchez.

"While I can never be one hundred percent certain of any diagnosis, I'd say someone put a curse on him designed to atrophy his heart muscle—and rather quickly."

Dr. Sanchez remained stoic, but from the way her hands were slightly shaking, I'd upset her. "Magic. You're sure?"

Hadn't I just said I was almost positive? "The stone turned yellow. Very yellow. That means a witch or warlock did this."

Her lips pressed together. "The last spell I encountered was the one put on Nash. That one was so powerful."

"Thankfully, we were able to figure out how to counteract the spell on Nash. Obviously, it's too late for your ex-husband."

She huffed. "Sadly, that's true. Could you tell if the person was standing close to Daniel when the spell was enacted—or whatever you call it? The answer might help determine who could have done this."

"It's called invoking a spell. That's an excellent question. I know nothing about a spell this strong, but for something this deadly, our resident psychic, Gertrude Poole, or more likely her grandson, Levy, together with his coven, might know."

"His group helped find the cure for Nash, right?"

"Yes. They are an amazing resource. Their extensive library is sure to hold some information about this."

It was always possible that Bertha Murdoch, who ran the Hex and Bones Apothecary, would know something, too. She'd been around forever. Having so many options upped our chances of success.

"I appreciate it, but please keep Daniel's name out of it for now—for Gavin's sake."

"For sure," I said.

"We need to move fast since I'm not sure Steve will give Nash the go ahead to investigate. At the moment, we can't prove Daniel was murdered, and without the autopsy saying it wasn't death by natural causes, there will be no investigation."

Then why did Steve drive the six hours to Miami? "If you've never seen a heart turn black before, surely that is cause for further study."

"Maybe, but we have to follow the law. I'll let Nash know what you found out, but the other medical examiner will not sign off on it as being murder unless the tox screens come back and show something."

I clasped her arm. "We'll get to the bottom of it." Though I wasn't sure if I was speaking for The Pink Iguana Sleuths or the sheriff's department.

"Thank you, Glinda." She looked up at Jaxson. "And to you, too."

Believing Rihanna, Gavin, and his stepmother needed more time alone, we returned to my place instead of stopping back at the office. To my surprise, Iggy was there.

"Had enough of the drama?" I asked.

"I couldn't stand that woman."

"Are you speaking about Morgana Sanchez?"

"What do you think? The only other woman there was Rihanna."

And Iggy loved her. I slipped off my coat and tossed it over the back of the sofa.

"How about I make us some coffee?" Jaxson suggested.

"That would be great. I'm still a bit chilled." January and February were the coldest months in Florida.

Iggy moved away from me. "You stink, you know."

"That's what happens when I go to the morgue. Before I shower, tell me what you learned."

"While Gavin's dad ate too much and had too much stress in his life—being a divorce lawyer and all—his wife thinks someone did him in."

Iggy had my interest. "Did Mrs. Sanchez say who she suspected?"

"I don't remember names, but she said something about a gardener. Then she suggested her sister might have killed him."

Morgana must not be close to her sister if she made such an accusation. "Did Mrs. Sanchez happen to mention if either of the suspects was a witch or a warlock?"

"No. And I didn't ask."

He'd have no reason to. Even I hadn't learned witchcraft was involved until a few minutes ago. "Did Mrs. Sanchez say why she thought one of them wanted to harm her husband?"

Jaxson came out of the kitchen carrying two cups of coffee. He set both on the coffee table and then sat in the chair across from me. "I heard something about a gardener and a sister?"

I repeated what Iggy told me.

Iggy lifted his head to let us know he was the special one for learning something new. "Mrs. Sanchez's sister works in the same law office as Daniel Sanchez. I think she liked him."

I looked over at Jaxson. "Could the sister have wanted Daniel, and when Morgana landed him instead, she couldn't handle it?"

"We could probably come up with a lot of reasons for someone wanting to harm another person. What's not to say that when Daniel made partner in the law firm that the sister believed she was the one who deserved the position more? Maybe the sister killed Daniel in the hopes it would pave the way for her advancement."

I huffed. "I see your point. I should start by making a list of suspects. Maybe Dolly's sister-in-law can check some of them out for us."

He blew on the steaming coffee and then sipped it. "Sounds good." He then turned to my familiar. "Any other tidbits that were interesting, Detective Iggy?"

Chapter Four

IGGY SCRATCHED HIS head, looking as if he was thinking. "The only other thing I learned was that Gavin seemed confused as to why his dad would come here and then not contact him."

That kind of rejection would hurt a lot, but Gavin had already mentioned that to us. "I think the dad's lack of contact should be our main concern. Why come and not tell anyone?"

"Could he have believed someone was trying to kill him, and he decided to hide in Witch's Cove?" my familiar suggested.

"That has merit," I said. "I'm surprised he didn't stay with his parents in that case."

"He probably didn't want to put them at risk."

"Then he shouldn't have come to Witch's Cove at all."

"Someone must know his reasoning," Jaxson said.

"I bet that Morgana lady knows," Iggy threw in.

"I already asked her. She told us she thought her husband was at a conference in Tallahassee."

"Then I bet she could guess why he lied," Iggy added.

"You might be right, though she probably would be more forthcoming with Gavin than with either of us."

"I agree with you," Jaxson said. "From her point of view, there is no reason for us to be snooping. If we ask too many questions, Morgana will want to know why we're so interested. Knowing you, you'll say that you believe he was murdered."

"But I do believe someone killed him."

"And what will Morgana ask you next when you say that?"

I could see where he was going with this. "Why would I think that, if a medical examiner couldn't figure it out?" I lifted my coffee, but it was a bit too hot to drink still. "Why can't I say I think a witch's spell killed her husband? It's the truth. If she laughs at me, then she laughs at me. At least, I would have told her."

"What if she is a witch? Or knows someone who is? What if Morgana confronts this person and ends up dead herself? How would that make you feel?"

Ugh. My partner's imagination was so out of control. "Fine. I'll say that his heart was so bad that it was the only explanation for his death."

"That would imply death by natural causes. Not murder."

"It would, wouldn't it?" My mind was mush. "I have to tell her what I really believe then."

"Before you say something you'll regret, how about we wait until after you speak with Levy or Gertrude? They might say no witch could have done such a thing."

"But my pendant—"

He smiled—sort of. "Turned yellow. I know. I just don't want what happened to Daniel Sanchez happening to you."

Jaxson always was looking out for me. "Fine. I'll say nothing. For now."

He flashed me a real smile this time. "You don't have to sound so despondent. It's for your own good."

I chuckled. "I know. It's just that you're always the one who's making sure I get out of my own way." I didn't like needing a protector. I just liked having one on standby.

"That's what partners are for." He polished off his drink. "I'm going to head home, but I'll be at the office tomorrow morning."

"I'll give Levy a call now. He might have heard of this type of curse and be able to give us some guidance."

Jaxson leaned over and kissed me. "Good luck."

As soon as he left, I sank back against the sofa. Even though witchcraft was most likely involved in this crime, I felt out of my element, which was dumb, since I was a witch, just not a very experienced one.

At least Levy had a lot more magical abilities than I did. He also had a coven at his fingertips. Swallowing my pride, I retrieved my phone and called him.

"Glinda! Nice to hear from you."

From his cheerful tone, he must not have heard about Gavin's father. I shouldn't be surprised since Levy lived two towns over. I explained about the odd circumstances of Daniel Sanchez's appearance here, and then how I thought he died. "My necklace turned solid yellow. There was no indecision at all."

"Hmm. How can I help?"

"The coroner can't put magic as the cause of death. For my own sake, I was hoping you or your coven might be able to confirm that my stone wasn't imagining things."

He chuckled. "I doubt your necklace has feelings."

"I know, but maybe the color yellow means something else besides magic. I don't want to get this wrong. We need the sheriff to believe this is a murder investigation."

"I understand, though it might not do any good if all we can come up with is the same witchcraft theory."

"I know, but Steve trusts you. He might investigate without corroboration from the medical examiner if the two of us say the same thing."

"Fine. I'll set up a meeting for you with a few of the members for tomorrow. Meeting them face to face is often better than email anyway. Do you think you could get a photo of the heart?"

"Eww. Why?"

"It might look familiar to one of them."

I would do anything I could to help. "Of course."

As soon as we set up a time to meet, I texted Dr. Sanchez and asked if she could send me the image. I explained why, hoping she didn't think I'd asked because I liked looking at gross stuff.

To my delight, a few minutes later, I received the image, which I immediately forwarded to Levy. I hoped that by sending it to me, that Dr. Sanchez was convinced someone had killed her ex-husband, and that witchcraft might have been the cause.

Once I met with Levy's coven, I would go over their findings with Dr. Sanchez, who may or may not share that knowledge with the medical examiner. Then I'd question her about Daniel's habits. I bet she knew more about her ex-husband than even she realized.

Gavin would also be a good source since both he and his dad lived in Miami until recently.

I turned off my phone. "I'm going to clean up," I announced to Iggy.

"About time. Maybe you could carry a bottle of perfume with you if you go to the morgue again."

I kept forgetting what a sensitive nose he had. "I'll try to come up with a solution."

"I appreciate it. I'm going to see what Aimee is up to," he said.

Aimee was my aunt's cat who, like Iggy, had the ability to speak. He fancied her as his girlfriend, but Aimee didn't always reciprocate the affection. "Good luck."

He swished his tail and waddled toward the cat door. I hoped she wasn't in one of her cat moods and snubbed Iggy. He needed her sympathy today. For all his bravado, Iggy seemed to be sincerely sorry for poor Gavin about his dad's death.

WHEN I PULLED up in front of the library around noon the next day where Levy and his coven held their meetings, my friend was outside waiting for me. I slipped out of the car, pulled my jacket around my shoulders, and greeted him.

"Thanks for helping. Again," I said.

Levy smiled. "Of course. We are always interested in ridding this world of bad witches and warlocks."

Just like the last time I was there, he used the palm print and then the eye scanner to open the door. Once inside, he led me to the eerily lit room that housed bookcases full of old magic books. I had to believe the library knew what was stored in here. Heck, I wouldn't be surprised if the librarian had magic and was part of the coven.

This time when I faced his crew, I wasn't nearly as intimidated. Instead of being greeted with a bit of suspicion like the last time, five people were there pouring over books, mostly ignoring me, for which I was grateful. I needed them focused.

Camila, the werewolf-witch hybrid looked up and smiled. "Hey, Glinda. Nice to see you again."

I wasn't sure why she would be happy to spend time away from her job, but maybe she and the others liked a mystery as much as I did. "You, too."

Levy reintroduced me to the group. When I was here before, he'd told me their names, but I'd forgotten a couple of them. My stress level at the time had been sky high.

"Have you found anything useful?" Levy asked his coven.

Diego looked up from the book he'd been studying and leaned back in his chair. "We were all intrigued by the sudden transformation, or rather deterioration, of the heart. It led us down some interesting dead ends, but we finally found one reference to the spell."

My pulse jumped. I pulled out a chair and sat down. "May I see?" He turned the book around.

"That looks like this man's heart. Do you know anything about the nature of the spell that caused it? Or how long it took to kill the person?"

Knowing how the spell was delivered might give me a clue about who could have done this. It would also make a difference if the spell caused instant heart failure, or if it took days or even weeks to disintegrate the cell walls. If it was quick acting, then the witch, or warlock, would have to be close by in Witch's Cove at the time of Daniel's death.

"The one we found takes about four or five days," Diego said.

That wasn't good. It opened it up to too many suspects. "I wonder if Daniel suffered a lot before his death."

"That I couldn't say, but from the pictures, I would think he might have."

"If he sought medical help, the doctor might be able to give us a clue what was going on—assuming Daniel was aware of the spell at the time," I said.

"That's a good place to start," Levy said. "Maybe it's why he came to Witch's Cove in the first place. He didn't want anyone in his home town to learn about his condition."

"No offense to my town, but I've never heard of a world-renowned cardiologist in Witch's Cove. He'd have better luck in Gainesville or Tampa." On the other hand, if he believed that someone had put a spell on him, he might think a witch could help more than a doctor.

"Then what about his ex-wife? She's a medical doctor. He might trust her to be discreet."

I really appreciated his different point of view. "Perhaps, but why not call or text her once he arrived? Considering the condition of his heart, he must have been feeling worse and worse by the day. At some point, he'd want to ask for her opinion."

"True."

"One thing I know for sure is that you need to be careful," Diego warned. "You don't want this witch or warlock to do the same to you if they think you are getting too close to the truth."

I shivered at that thought, even though I'd considered that possibility—or rather Jaxson had. "Scare me much?" I chuckled, but there was no joy in any of this. "That leads me to my next question. In your research, did any of you come across any kind of protection spell to prevent something like this from happening to me?"

"Not yet," Camila said. "We will definitely look for a countermeasure. It might take us a few days to find it, though."

These guys were great. "I appreciate it."

After chatting a bit more, but learning nothing new, Levy escorted me out. "You will stay safe, right?"

He sounded worried. To be honest, I was also concerned. "Yes. I made a list of my suspects, and I'll try to steer clear of them. I just wish I could tell if someone is a witch or warlock."

"Assume everyone is, and that way you'll stay alive."

I chuckled. "If only it were that easy. I owe you one!"

He smiled. "Anytime."

As soon as I was in the car, I called Jaxson to see if he'd like to meet at Maude's tea shop to chat.

"I'd love to. Rihanna is still with Gavin, and I feel like I'm a third wheel."

"I get it. See you in a few then."

I started the car and headed to town. No surprise, Jaxson was at the tea shop when I walked in. On the table was my usual sweet tea, along with a chocolate chip cookie—my favorite.

I sat opposite him. "You are the best."

"I try. What did you find out?"

I gave him a brief rundown. "I won't learn what anyone can do to protect us for a few days. And that's assuming there is something that can be done."

He took a drink from his coffee cup. "If a witch put a spell on Mr. Sanchez, that person is pure evil. You have to be careful."

"I will be."

The bell above the door dinged and Betty Sanchez came in, looking rather gaunt. Betty and her husband, Frank, owned Candle's Bookstore, a place where I'd spent many hours when I was in high school. They were also Daniel Sanchez's parents.

Betty didn't even glance our way as she headed to a table in the corner. The poor woman looked so lost. I thought her husband would be with her, but I suppose someone had to man the store, even though I'm sure everyone in town would understand if they closed it for a few days. Knowing Frank, he needed to stay open for his own sanity—or else there was no love lost between him and his son.

"I think I'll go over and offer my sympathies," I said.

"That is nice of you. What are you going to ask her?"

Was I that obvious? Most likely yes. "I'll figure it out when I get over there."

Before Jaxson convinced me it was a bad idea, I pushed back my chair and walked over to her table.

Betty looked up and gave me a brief half smile. "Glinda."

I sat down at her table. "I wanted to say how terribly sorry I am for your loss. It had to be such a shock."

"In all honesty, it wasn't totally unexpected. My son was a troubled man."

Whoa. I hadn't expected that comment. Did she think he took his own life? Considering the condition of his heart, I don't think he could have done that to himself. "I don't understand."

She leaned forward as if to tell me a secret. "That new wife of his was bankrupting him. It was driving him to desperation."

That almost proved Morgana had nothing to do with her new husband's death. She wouldn't want her golden goose to die. "He was in financial trouble?" Neither Gavin nor Morgana even hinted at that possibility.

"Yes. He couldn't afford that witch. Morgana spent money like it was water."

I almost whistled. A witch? I had to assume that was just a figure of speech. "Did Daniel come to Witch's Cove to see if Elissa would be willing to lend him money?"

"I don't know."

"I don't believe he ever spoke with her."

"Of course, he did."

Okay, someone wasn't telling the truth. Perhaps Elissa didn't want Gavin to know about his father's financial woes and told him she wasn't aware he was in town. "I had no idea. I'm sorry."

When tears welled in Betty's eyes, I thought I'd stirred up enough emotions for now. It was time to rejoin Jaxson.

Chapter Five

"WHAT DID BETTY say?" Jaxson asked as I sat back down at the tea shop table. I explained about Daniel possibly being in financial trouble. "If that was the case, why was he planning a trip abroad?"

"Good question. Too many things aren't adding up. I want to know why Elissa denied seeing Daniel, assuming he wasn't the one who lied."

"Are you going to confront Elissa about it?"

"You might be surprised to hear that I don't plan to do that. If she needs to keep something a secret, I'm sure she has her reasons."

He whistled. "Wow. I'm impressed. My Glinda Goodall is growing up."

I let my mouth drop open. "Growing up? Are you implying I've been immature? I'm twenty-seven."

He grinned. "Just saying that you seem more…cautious in your old age."

Old age? He was older than me by a few years. Maybe that was why since meeting Jaxson, I often thought before I acted. Jaxson's cautious nature must be wearing off on me. "That's a good thing."

"It is. So, tell me, cautious one, was there anything else

you learned with your meeting with Levy's coven?" Jaxson must not think the other information all that relevant.

I blew out a breath. "Nothing much. Like I said, it might be days to find how to counteract this heart-hardening spell or protect against it. Obviously, it's too late for Daniel, but what if it happens again?"

"To you?"

"Yes, to me. Or Rihanna. Or you! If I ask one wrong question, that witch or warlock could come after us."

"That would hamper our investigation," he said.

"I'm serious."

"So am I," Jaxson said with a sparkle in his eye.

"I'm hoping the coven will find some protective spell to put around all of us."

"Let's make sure they do before we land in the killer's crosshairs."

"I'm depending on it."

"What's next on the agenda then?" he asked.

I'd thought about that on the way back from meeting with the coven. "I want to tell Elissa about the curse we found. If she knows it was in some ancient tome, she might be more cautious. The killer could believe she knows some-thing—even though she doesn't. At least no more than we do. If Daniel didn't speak with her, he might have come to see another medical professional. Elissa might know of a doctor who could have checked Daniel out."

"And if she knows nothing?"

I scrunched up my nose. "Roadblocks. I hate them." I snapped my fingers. "I'll give Dolly the names of Morgana's sister and the gardener in the hopes her sister-in-law can get the scoop on them."

"That's a long shot, but worth a try. Do you know their names?"

I pointed a finger at him. "Not yet, but that is where Gavin comes in. If he hasn't met his dad's gardener or his stepmother's sister, I bet he can find out their names from Morgana."

"Sounds good."

"Not only that, but Gavin might be able to give us some insight into his dad's comings and goings, assuming that kind of conversation isn't too painful for him."

Jaxson shook his head. "It might not be. I wasn't eaves-dropping on purpose, but Gavin's voice travels, even through a closed bedroom door. I got the sense there was a fair amount of friction between father and son. It might have been why Gavin decided to spend a year in Witch's Cove."

"Then we should thank Daniel—posthumously, of course—for sending Gavin our way. He's been just what Rihanna needed to feel like she belonged here."

"I agree."

Once we finished up and paid, we headed back to the office. I would have asked Maude what she knew about the murder, but it was her day off. Whenever one of the five gossip queens wasn't around, it put a crimp in our crime solving ability.

When we arrived at the office, Iggy was there, as were Rihanna and Gavin, only now they were in the main room—without Morgana. "Hey," I said.

They halted their conversation, and I could only hope we hadn't interrupted something serious.

"How did it go with Levy's coven?" Rihanna asked.

They both knew that I believed Gavin's dad had a spell put on him. Rihanna believed me, but I wasn't as sure about Gavin. "One of the members found what appeared to be the same spell in some ancient book."

I loved that Rihanna's eyes lit up. "Can we stop this person?"

"They couldn't find a way to counteract the spell yet, but a protection spell might exist. When they locate it, I want all of us to get it."

"Even me?" Gavin asked.

"Absolutely." I sat down and motioned everyone else to join me. "Look, if I'm wrong, and some magical person didn't put a spell on your dad, then it won't matter."

"I guess not."

"How does this heart-killing spell work?" Rihanna asked.

I explained that it could last up to five days before the person died.

Gavin was tapping his foot, making me more anxious. Rihanna placed a hand on his leg, and he stopped. Having a mind reader in the family was useful at times.

I mentally thanked Rihanna, but whether she received the message or not, I couldn't tell.

"That means someone in Miami could have done this to him," Gavin said.

"It would seem that way. Since he doesn't know anyone here other than you, your mom, and your grandparents, it kind of makes sense."

"I guess, but how can we find him—or her?" he asked.

I hissed in a breath. "I don't think we should do anything

until Steve returns, and we hear back from the coven. It's too dangerous to go to Miami and be subject to the same kind of spell should we get too close to the killer. I've started a list of possible suspects, but I'd like your input, Gavin."

"Sure. Anything." Gavin looked over at Rihanna and then back at us. "If we go to Miami, I think Rihanna should stay here, though. I don't want anything to happen to her."

The sentiment warmed my heart. "I might agree, except that Rihanna is the only one of the four of us who can read minds, more or less."

Rihanna looked up at him. "Maybe you should stay, Gavin. This could be a vendetta against your family."

He shook his head. "I don't think so. It would surprise me if many people even knew my dad had a son."

Gavin had to be exaggerating, but maybe it was true. "Don't assume you're in the clear. It's always possible someone wanted to take revenge on your family. Besides, your father could have a photo of you on his desk. You'd be easy to track down, what with social media the way it is these days."

He shrugged. "I guess. I appreciate you all wanting to make sure I stay safe, but I have to be the one to go. I know Miami. Dad talked about the people he worked with all the time. I might not have met them all, but I have a good sense of who they are."

"He has a point, Glinda," Jaxson said.

"Fine." I grabbed a pad of paper. "Morgana mentioned that her sister, who worked with your dad, might have harmed him. Do you know her name?"

"Yes. It's Sandra Cortez."

"Do you think she's capable of harming your father?"

"Are you asking me if she's a witch?"

"I guess she'd have to be."

He shook his head. "No way."

People never suspected I was one for the longest time either. "Did you know Rihanna was a witch the first time you met her?"

He glanced to the side. "No. Okay. Fine. Sandra could be a witch. She's ruthless enough. Sorry. I didn't mean to imply all witches are ruthless." He lifted Rihanna's hand and brought her fingers to his lips.

"No offense taken," I shot back. "What about your dad's gardener?"

"Mauricio? No way. He's a real nice guy. He's a genius when it comes to landscape design."

"Does this genius have a last name?"

Gavin glanced at the ceiling. "Jimenez. He's from Mexico or some Spanish speaking country."

I scribbled down the information. "If you had to guess who might have wanted your father dead, who would that be?"

Gavin shrugged. "He didn't talk much about his cases. He said it was lawyer-client privileged information stuff."

"How about the people he worked with?" Jaxson asked. "Besides Morgana's sister, would anyone else have it out for your dad?"

"He won a lot of cases. Someone might have been jealous of his many successes."

If he won so many cases, how was he broke? Secondly, would a smart, sophisticated fifty-year-old man be okay with his new wife purchasing so many things that she bankrupted him? While I hated to burden Gavin further, I wanted to make sure that Betty's facts were right. "Your grandmother said that your father was experiencing financial difficulties."

He barked out a laugh. "Dad? No way. Why would she say that?"

"I don't know. Maybe your father told them that for a reason. Betty said he spent a lot of money on Morgana."

"That wasn't true. I don't like her at all, but she came from a very wealthy family. She didn't need my dad's money if that's what you're thinking."

Okay that messed up every theory I ever had. "That is interesting. If you think of anyone else, let me know, and I'll add their name to the list."

"Will do."

"We should find out when Steve is returning," Jaxson said.

I pulled out my phone. "Nash will know. It can't take that long for him to coordinate a plan with the Miami police."

"Wait until he hears witchcraft is involved," Rihanna added. "Both he and Nash will be beside themselves."

"I don't envy Steve if we convince him the real cause of Gavin's father's death was because of magic." I dialed Nash's number, and he answered rather quickly.

"Glinda."

"Hey, Nash. Do you know when Steve will be returning from Miami?"

"Why?"

I disliked the word *why*—except when I used it. "I'm just curious if he found out anything."

"Elissa told me about your theory."

I bristled at the word *theory*. "I can send you the image of the heart so you can see for yourself."

"She already sent me the copy. I will admit it does appear that witchcraft could be involved. Knowing you, you have a plan to find this person."

I let out a long breath. "Yes. I spoke with Levy's coven to see if they could point me in the right direction."

"And?"

It had been Levy's group who had provided me with the spell to treat Nash. Without their help, Nash would be dead. "They found the spell, but they aren't sure how to prevent it from occurring to anyone else, nor have they found a way to protect others from being affected. They will let me know if they learn something."

"I hope that means you won't do anything until Steve returns."

He was smart. "That's my plan."

"Good. Steve will be back tomorrow."

I smiled. "Thank you."

"Anytime. Please, keep me in the loop. No one should have this happen to them like what Daniel Sanchez went through."

"I couldn't agree more."

I disconnected and told them what our deputy said.

"Once the sheriff returns, suppose he knows nothing," Gavin said. "Then what?"

"Good question. Once we figure out a way to be immune to this terrible spell, I want to take a road trip to Miami. First, though, I'll ask Dolly to ask her sister-in-law to check out the gardener and Morgana's sister. I'm not sure what she'll learn, but maybe she'll surprise us."

"When do you expect to hear back from Levy?" Rihanna asked.

"They seemed very determined to find an answer quickly."

She smiled. "Then I guess we wait."

"What about Morgana?" Jaxson asked.

"What about her?" I asked.

"Should we tell her we plan to go down to Miami and ask around?"

That might be smart if we were positive she had nothing to do with Daniel Sanchez's death. For all we know, she is the witch with a secret motive. "Not yet." I turned to Gavin. "Are you okay with not telling her right away?"

"Of course. I don't trust her. Never have. She twists everything and makes it all about her."

I really didn't want to get into that discussion, so I stood. "As soon as I learn something from the coven, we'll present it to Steve and Nash, and then we'll plan our trip to Miami."

"It's funny," Gavin said. "I'm almost looking forward to going back, and here I thought I never wanted to see that city again."

"Why is that?" Rihanna asked.

"Because of all the disagreements I had with dad. Don't get me wrong, we had some good times. Maybe if I visit, I can pretend he's still alive."

That would be great if it helped. "Hopefully, someone will know who wanted to harm your father," I said.

"Even if we find out who killed him, my father isn't coming back." His voice faded away.

"No, but we can stop this person from doing this to any-one else."

"Glinda," Jaxson said. "How can you promise that?"

Darn. I couldn't. "We'll figure out a way."

Jaxson grabbed his laptop and motioned we leave. Regard-less of our odds, I had a good feeling about this upcoming trip.

Chapter Six

"I FOUND SOMETHING," Jaxson called from my kitchen table.

I rushed in. "What is it?"

He turned his computer toward me. "This is a picture of Morgana's sister, Sandra Cortez."

She was dressed in a very conservative blue suit, and her dark auburn hair was pulled back into a bun. "Very put together. That's her corporate photo, I take it?"

"It is." He clicked on another tab. "And this is from some junior staff member's social media site."

I studied the picture. "That's her?"

"Yup. She looks different, doesn't she?"

Sandra's hair was down. While her slacks and spiked heels looked expensive, like something a successful lawyer might wear, she looked young and happy. "Is she hanging all over Gavin's dad or what?"

"That seems to be the case."

He clicked on a few more photos that I bet Sandra had no idea even existed. I whistled. "It would appear that she liked her brother-in-law. A lot."

"I agree. I'll save these to my phone. When we talk to her—after we've received our protection spell—we'll ask her about them."

"Are you going with the theory that she was in love with her co-worker and was jealous that her sister landed him instead? She then decided to get back at Morgana by killing Daniel?" I asked.

"I don't know what to think. Right now, I'm merely collecting information."

That was a good approach. If the two sisters were at odds with each other though, why not kill the sister and have Daniel for herself? That might imply Daniel snubbed Sandra. Having too many options always frustrated me. "Did you look into Mauricio Jimenez, gardener extraordinaire?"

"I did. You will not believe what I found out about him."

I pulled out the chair and sat down. "Tell me."

"When I typed in his name, all I found was a photo of Mauricio living in Mexico at the time."

I leaned over. "Nice looking guy."

"Hey."

"But this man is dressed in medical scrubs. Hardly the attire for a gardener. Are you sure you found the right person?"

"I wasn't sure until I translated what it said about him. The translator app was a bit off, but I understood the gist. Apparently, Mauricio was a doctor who decided to leave Mexico and move to Florida, even though he knew that once in the United States, if he ever wanted to practice again, he'd have to get re-certified."

"Who would do that then?"

"It might have been a political thing."

I tried to make sense of it all. "Maybe someone found out

he was a warlock and reported him. He could have been forced to leave."

"I won't dismiss anything just yet. Let's suppose this guy had been a doctor and was willing to give it up to move here. What motive would he have for killing Daniel Sanchez, the man who hired him?"

"I'd only be guessing, but if Morgana was the one with the money, Mauricio might have wanted her. Get rid of the husband, and the way to the wife becomes easier." Without any facts, it was like closing my eyes and trying to play darts.

"I'll do a little more digging."

"Sounds good. Did Gavin say when his stepmother was leaving Witch's Cove and returning to Miami?" I asked.

"No, but I imagine she'll want to make arrangements to have the body transferred back home. Even if she plans to have him cremated, I imagine she'll have to stay for a couple more days since she can't sign out the body until the autopsy is complete."

"Agreed. I'll text Rihanna and see if Gavin can ask Morgana about the gardener. She did say she suspected him. I wonder why?"

"Tell him to be subtle," Jaxson warned.

"Do you think Morgana could be a witch or the gardener a warlock for that matter?"

He shrugged. "I'm not discounting anyone."

"Smart. I'll warn Gavin, but I'll suggest to Rihanna that she try to read Mrs. Sanchez's mind, if she hasn't already."

"Rihanna can't tell if Morgana is a witch, can she?"

"Not that I know of, but Rihanna might be able to tell if Morgana thinks witchy thoughts."

"Witchy thoughts?"

I smiled. "You know what I mean."

"I do. Just teasing you, pink lady."

THE NEXT MORNING at the office, my cell rang. Rihanna was at school, and I had to guess that Gavin was with his mom, so I wasn't sure who it could be. Only one way to find out—check the caller ID.

"It's Levy," I told Jaxson who was sitting at the desk next to mine.

"Great. Answer it."

That would be helpful. "Hey, Levy."

"We found something."

My whole body tensed, but in a good way. "Is it about the protection spell?"

"It is. I'm visiting my grandmother right now. Mind if I stop by the office in a few, assuming you're going to be there?"

"Jaxson and I will both be here."

"Rihanna is at school, right?"

"Yes." I didn't know if he wished she had been back here or not.

"Good. See you soon." He then disconnected.

I turned to Jaxson. "That was rather odd. Levy is stopping over. He and or his coven found a protection spell."

"That's great, but why is that odd?"

"I don't know. He kind of sounded worried."

"Worried how?"

"I'm not sure. Like the spell might involve something we

won't like." I pushed back my chair. "If he's on his way, I want to brew some tea for him."

Jaxson chuckled. "You do that."

He must think I'm crazy for being anxious. I believed in witchcraft. I really did, but I wasn't positive some ancient spell could work against someone this powerful, and if it didn't work, this little trip to Miami could endanger all of our lives. Unfortunately, I didn't have a choice. I was certain Daniel's death was a result of witchcraft, and no Miami police officer stood a chance against this person.

While I mulled over whether going to Miami with Rihanna and Gavin was the right move, I brewed the tea. Once I finished, I let it cool. Only after Levy arrived, would I toss in some ice.

Before I had the chance to return to the main room, someone knocked. "I'll get it," I called to Jaxson.

I rushed to the door and pulled it open. Not only was Levy there, but so was Levy's ninety-year old grandmother, Gertrude, who was holding onto the railing, panting.

Levy half chuckled. "May we come in?"

"Sorry." My mouth must have opened. I stepped to the side. As soon as Gertrude came through the door, I slipped an arm through hers. "Long way up, huh?"

"Very long. You need an elevator."

It sounded as if Iggy had put her up to mentioning the need for one. Even if he had, she'd deny ever conferring with him. She loved my familiar. Speaking of which, I wonder where he was? I hadn't seen him in a few hours.

I'd just closed the door when who should pop in through the cat door but my sassy familiar—an iguana who was not out of breath. Ten bucks said he and Gertrude conferred on their way up here.

He looked up at me, stilled, and then started to hyperventilate. "Long way up," he panted.

"Too late, buddy. I'm onto your game."

Jaxson was already on his feet. He wrapped an arm around Gertrude's waist, and I let go. He led her to the sofa.

She waved him off. "I can walk. I'm not dead yet."

"How about some iced tea?"

"I'd love some. Thanks." I looked over at Levy, and he nodded.

While those two settled in, I rushed to get the drinks. A moment later, I returned and set the tray on the coffee table. "Tell me about this protection spell."

Levy looked over at his grandmother. "It's a little bit different from the usual kind of spell. In fact, it's a lot different," Levy said.

"I don't understand."

"What my grandson is trying to say is that certain people are immune to the evil spell already. There's no incantation to say that will protect against it. Either you are immune or you're not."

Gertrude acted as if that explained it all. "I still don't understand."

She was about to continue when Levy placed a hand on her arm. "Here's the bottom line. The only way to be protected from this black-heart death spell is to be with someone you love when the spell is invoked."

Tea dribbled down my chin from my jaw dropping open once more. I swiped off the liquid with the back of my hand.

"What are you talking about? I've never even heard of anything like that. Furthermore, that doesn't sound like witchcraft to me."

Levy held up a hand. "None of us had heard of it before, but the passage is clear. Like I said, if you are in love—and loving a pet or a parent doesn't count—then you are immune to this black-heart spell, assuming you are with this person at the time the curse is invoked."

Wow. I looked over at Jaxson. He reached out and grabbed my hand. "I guess I'm safe then," he announced with a huge grin.

I nearly crumbled. Was he saying he loved me? I mean, he acted like he did, but I didn't want to get my hopes up. It was why I never put a label on how I felt toward him.

Jaxson dipped his chin, clearly waiting for me to tell him, but what if he was only kidding?

Stop it, Glinda. I know my own mind. "Me, too."

Levy beamed. "Great."

I didn't dare look at Jaxson. "What about Rihanna and Gavin? They aren't here. I know my cousin adores Gavin, but is that true love? She's only eighteen." I was babbling, I know.

"Relax, Glinda. I know Rihanna. Young love or real love. It doesn't matter. If they stay by each other's side, they will be protected," Gertrude said.

I looked over at Levy. "Really? Are you sure one of your coven members didn't want to admit defeat and just made this up?"

"No, she didn't. I promise you. We found the same information in two different sources." Levy glanced at Jaxson. "Is she always like this?"

That snapped me out of my namby-pamby attitude. I sat up straighter. "No. This talk of love temporarily short-circuited my brain. But don't worry. I have total faith in my relationship with Jaxson." It was the idea that being in love would actually protect us against this other spell that sounded a bit far-fetched to me.

Levy smiled. "Good."

"What should I tell Rihanna?" I asked.

Gertrude smiled. "Send her over to me. I'll explain it to her. We see eye-to-eye."

That meant they would engage in that mind-reading trick with each other. "I'll tell her to stop by after school."

"You do that."

Levy polished off his tea. "Thanks. And good luck finding the witch or warlock who needs to be taken down."

"What should we do if we find this person? It's not like we can have him arrested. Even with a confession, no court in the world would convict him. The law doesn't believe in magic."

I realized there were courts for witches and such, but proving the person invoked a particular spell would be impossible to prove.

Levy smiled. "Leave that to me and my coven."

Excitement raced through me. "What do you mean?"

"I think there is a way to destroy this person's ability to ever use the spell again. It won't put the person in jail for murder, but it will prevent him from ever harming anyone again using this magic."

"That might be worse than being in jail."

"Let's hope so," Levy said.

"What do you have to do to take away this person's power?" I imagine it would take some serious witchcraft abilities.

"If I tell you, I'd have to kill you," he said out of the side of his mouth.

Indignation shot up my spine. "You have to be kidding."

Levy cracked up. "Of course, I'm kidding. I've always wanted to say that line, and you handed me the perfect opportunity. Seriously, to basically kill a person's magical ability like that, it will take several of us to perform a coordinated spell."

"Coordinated? Will you have to capture him and hold him under water for three minutes, all the while sprinkling fairy dust on him as you chant in some ancient tongue?" I was being ridiculous, but to eliminate such a powerful person's ability would require drastic measures.

Levy shook his head while he huffed out a laugh. "You really need to book some appointments with my grandmother to learn the rudiments of magic."

That was just plain insulting, especially since if he'd read my mind just then, he'd know I was joking. "I'm good. I don't really believe in fairy dust anyway."

"Oh, really? Actually, that part is correct. It's the near drowning that is not. As for chanting in some ancient tongue, we just politely ask the witch's abilities to leave."

"Okay, joking aside, what needs to happen to cancel out this person's magic?" I tried to sound professional.

He sobered. "We're still working on it, but we'll need to be in close proximity to the sorcerer—like within ten feet or so for it to work."

"We think the perpetrator lives in Miami." Which meant

Levy and his coven members would have to drive down there if we found him.

"Then we'll go there." He stood and helped up his grandmother.

Gertrude turned to me. "We can start with some basic spells whenever you're ready."

I hope she was kidding, too. I'd taken some lessons from her already, and my last spell had reversed a curse put on Nash. I might have had some help, but in the end, he was cured. "I'll sign up as soon as I return from Miami." Or not.

"You do that, Glinda."

With that, the two of them left.

As soon as I closed the door behind them, I almost didn't want to turn around. Had I just professed my love for Jaxson Harrison? To be fair, he'd said it first, but that didn't really matter. Over the last nine months, he'd become more and more dear to me—not only as a business partner, but as a friend and major supporter. So what was my problem?

Two hands clasped my shoulders and turned me around. "We need to talk about this, and you know it."

Why couldn't he be like the typical guy who avoided all things emotional? When I'd first met him, I was fifteen, and he was this twenty-one year old, muscular stud who had the biggest chip on his shoulder. That guy wouldn't tell a woman he liked her if he had a gun to his head.

I guess he grew up.

"Talk about what? How cool it is that we are immune?"

Jaxson moved closer, if that was possible, and peered down at me. "It's the *why* we are immune part that is cool."

"It is."

Iggy waddled out from under the sofa. "I can go with you guys to Miami."

I spun to face him, happy for the distraction. "Why is that?"

"Because I love Aimee."

I couldn't believe Iggy would admit that. "That's great, but we aren't taking her with us."

"That's okay. I can still come."

"I think Levy said both parties have to be present for you to be immune, buddy," Jaxson said. "I'll have to be by Glinda's side the whole time we are there, or she could be harmed. Can you guarantee that Aimee won't wander off? She is a cat, after all."

Iggy looked up at me. "That's not what I got out of the conversation."

I did adore him. "How about if I ask Levy if the spell makes an exception for familiars?"

"Okay, but remember Aimee isn't a familiar."

I saluted him. "Got it."

Love? Seriously? That was the solution to the problem? Who would have guessed?

Chapter Seven

"READY TO HEAR what Steve learned from his trip to Miami?" I asked.

"I am."

Did Jaxson and I have *the talk* about love yet? Not really. Okay, not at all, but hey, I wasn't ready to have that discussion. It seemed so personal, but I would have to at some point. I hadn't proclaimed my love just to stay safe. I meant it, and I hoped he meant it, too.

We walked across the street to the sheriff's office where Pearl was manning the desk. She looked up and smile. "My, oh, my. This is a surprise!"

I don't know why. A murder had been committed. Considering magic was involved, it made sense we'd be here, but I didn't want to dampen her spirits by saying so. It was hard enough to stay upbeat after the unnecessary tragedy.

"Hey, Pearl, is Steve around?" I asked.

"He sure is. Nash has filled him in on your magical theory. I must say, it is intriguing but scary." Her eyes went from wide to narrow as if she was performing in front of a camera.

I wasn't sure how to respond, so I decided to remain noncommittal. "To us too."

Once we made it back to his office, we knocked, and

entered. Steve, our diligent sheriff, was leaning back in his chair looking really tired.

"How was the drive back?" I wanted to get a feel for his mood.

He sat up straighter. "Fine. Have a seat. I don't know how you do it, but it seems like I might be using your witchy services once more."

I mentally pumped a fist. "Does that mean you believe Daniel Sanchez was murdered by a witch or a warlock?"

"I have to say, it's a strong possibility." He took a sip from his coffee cup. "To be thorough, I spoke with Elissa about it, and she said that even that fast acting flesh-eating bacteria I've read about couldn't have been the cause of death since the medical examiner found no break in the skin where the bacteria would have entered."

"Good to know." I didn't need the details. I'd already seen the hardened heart, and it wasn't pretty. "What did the cops in Miami say?"

"When the Miami PD interviewed his co-workers, they all said that Sanchez was energetic and feeling well just a few days before his death. He didn't complain of a fever or anything, which implies something happened right before he left or right after he arrived in Witch's Cove. The medical examiner has not ruled out poison. He's awaiting the lab results now."

That was good that Dr. Alvarez was being thorough. "Considering the lack of physical evidence, did anyone on the Miami Force think Daniel Sanchez might have been murdered?" Had he been beaten up, it would be easier to go the murder route.

"Not really, but until the autopsy comes back, they won't

commit one way or the other."

"That's smart."

"And yes, the cops asked his co-workers and neighbors who might have wanted to harm him. A few names were batted about, and the Miami PD will follow up with these leads."

"Did they tell you who they suspected?"

"They had someone, but the man's been cleared. Apparently, Mr. Sanchez was being sued by the husband of a woman he represented. At first, the police thought the man might have wanted Mr. Sanchez dead."

"How do they know he was innocent?"

"Because Daniel Sanchez died in Witch's Cove, and this guy can prove he was in Miami at the time. That means if you take magic off the table, no one who was in Miami at the time of Sanchez's death will make the suspect list—at least not directly."

"I take it you didn't mention the idea of magic to them?"

Steve twirled the pencil in his right hand and smiled. "No. I think the police down south wouldn't have believed me even if I had."

"You're probably right. That means it's up to us to find the witch or warlock who is responsible. Even a sorcerer needs motive to kill—or so I believe."

"That might be true, but you even said you can't tell who is one and who isn't, so how do you plan on finding this person-of-magic?"

The title of *person-of-magic* had a nice ring to it. "We have to wait for him or her to slip up. If they don't, the sorcerer might get away with murder."

"That would be a real shame," Steve said.

"For sure. To be thorough, what was the name of the man who was suing Sanchez? And do you know why he was suing Gavin's dad?" I asked.

Steve lifted his trusty yellow pad and flipped through a few pages. "His name is Ed Whitlow. He is claiming Sanchez falsified papers in favor of Whitlow's ex-wife. Because of that, the court ruled in her favor for an exorbitant amount of alimony."

"What would have happened if Sanchez hadn't died and he'd lost the case?" I asked.

"I'm suspecting he'd have been suspended for six to twelve months."

"That would depress anyone. Sanchez might have come to Witch's Cove to tell his son what was happening, so he'd be prepared for the worst."

"That's plausible, but we may never learn the real reason for his trip. He never contacted Gavin, right?"

"No, he didn't."

Jaxson leaned forward. "Did Daniel Sanchez have a computer with him?"

Steve nodded. "He did, but we didn't find anything useful on it. We are not as technically sophisticated as you are, so if you want to take a look at it in our conference room, you're welcome to it."

Jaxson reached over and squeezed my leg. "I'll do that. Browser history can be a gold mine of information. Thank you."

"Glinda, what's your next move? I know you aren't capable of sitting back and waiting for me to solve the case. I'd like to know your plans."

By now, I was used to his barbs of me always interfering. "Like I said, we intend to find this person and bring him to justice if we can."

"And chance being killed, too?"

While it was a bit embarrassing to tell him why we couldn't be harmed, he needed to know. "Jaxson and I are immune to this evil spell."

A smile crossed Steve's lips. "Immune to being killed by this guy? Tell me how. I need a good laugh."

"There's nothing funny about it." I explained what Levy learned about this ancient ritual.

"You're telling me that if I admit to being in love with Misty, and she admits it to me, that we could go after this person with no chance of being harmed?"

It was one thing to put my life on the line, but to endanger Steve and the sheriff over in Liberty, was another. However, either I believed Levy was right or I didn't believe. "That's right, but when you admit it, you really have to mean it."

"Got it."

I waited for him to say he loved Misty, but apparently, he wasn't in the sharing mood.

"Just so you know, Jaxson, Rihanna, Gavin, and I plan to go on a road trip to Miami to see what we can find out."

"Have you ever been to Miami?" One brow rose.

Did that imply I'd get lost in the city or something? "No, but Gavin knows his way around, and Dolly's sister-in-law hangs out with some of Daniel's friends. She's discreetly checking her sources and will share with us what she's learned when we get there."

He nodded. "Sounds good, but in case things don't go as planned, I'll give Sergeant Bogart a call. He is the lead detective on our joint investigation. I doubt he believes in the spirit world, but I'll ask him to call me if you guys get into trouble."

"We plan to keep a low profile. I'm not so naïve to believe that just because this warlock won't be able to kill us with that heart-killing spell, that he can't harm us in other ways."

"Can't you strike back if he doles out another kind of magic?" He held out both hands and wiggled them while making some weird noise that sounded like electricity popping. "Like zap the guy using your mind or something?"

I chuckled. "I'm not a superhero."

"Are you sure? You did that spell to heal Nash. And you've done many other spells that helped find criminals. Why not this time?"

"I'll see what I can do. Thank you for your vote of confidence." I'd never produced any kind of electric spark, lit a fire with my mind, or harmed anything using thoughts, but I saw no reason to highlight my witch short-comings.

"You're welcome."

Jaxson and I said our goodbyes. Once we were out of the station, I faced him. "How about we grab a cup of coffee at the Bubbling Cauldron."

"Do you think Miriam will know something?"

"I doubt it. I just need a moment to think. I figure if Pearl had any gossip, she would have shared it already. I really think our gossip queens won't be of much help on this case."

"Other than Dolly's sister-in-law."

"Right. Let's hope she's as good as Dolly thinks she is."

We entered the shop, waved to Miriam who was with a customer, and found a table.

"I can see the wheels turning," Jaxson said.

By now, I wasn't surprised that he knew me so well. "Steve was right."

"About what?"

"I'm a witch. I need to learn to cast some special spell—an evil one to be exact—that will stop this person from harming us in any way, in case he has other talents."

"Didn't Levy say he knew of something to kill this guy's mojo?"

"Yes, but it will take him and his coven members half a day to drive down once we contact him. What if we need something to stop this person right away?"

"Are you thinking of asking for Gertrude's help?"

I shook my head. "She'd tell Levy. I was thinking Bertha might be better able to help."

"Then Bertha it is."

"When Rihanna gets back from speaking with Gertrude after school, the two of us will head on over and see what we can find. Having two witches is always better than one."

"Having your cousin in particular with you will be important since she can read that person's mind to see if he or she has evil intentions," Jaxson said.

"Exactly. We'll also need to come up with a cover story for why we are all in Miami."

Miriam came over and placed a hand on my shoulder. "How is Gavin holding up? I heard he's been spending a lot of time with Rihanna." She shook her head, genuinely looking upset. "I still can't believe Daniel is gone."

"It is quite the shock. I'm glad Gavin has someone to talk to, too." Her comment implied she knew Daniel Sanchez. "Had you met Daniel before?"

"A long time ago. He grew up in Witch's Cove."

Since his parents have lived in Witch's Cove for forever, I figured he must have grown up here. "When did he move away?"

"Oh, my. Years and years ago. After he graduated from high school, I think."

"I see. Thanks."

When I didn't give her any more information, she lifted her order pad. I asked for my usual iced coffee and a croissant, and Jaxson went with his standard black coffee. The man had discipline.

Once Miriam returned to the counter to fix our drinks, Jaxson studied me. "You can't be thinking someone from thirty years ago would seek revenge against Daniel, now would you?"

"Not really. I think our Miami connection is our best bet, but if we fail down there, we should do a little investigating into who might still be living here from that time."

"I can always pull up an old yearbook and look through the names."

I smiled. "I knew I liked having you around for a reason."

"Is that the only reason?" The side of his mouth quirked up.

"Of course, not." I hoped he wasn't about to bring up the topic of our profession of love. Before he could probe that minefield further, our drinks arrived.

For much of our coffee break, I tried to figure out if I was up for this trip. Going head-to-head against a powerful sorcerer was not my thing. Even if Bertha had a magnificent spell that would turn the evil person into stone for twenty seconds, allowing us to escape, I wouldn't trust myself to get the spell right, especially if I was under pressure. It didn't matter, I was getting better. Having Rihanna by my side—as well as Jaxson—would help.

"What do you think about asking Iggy to come with us? Mind you, that's assuming Levy tells me that my familiar won't be affected by the madman."

"How can he know for sure? I highly doubt the effect of this spell on an animal would be mentioned in an ancient tome."

"You're probably right," I said.

"On the other hand, Iggy has his uses. He can sneak into places unnoticed and report back to us."

"Iggy is good at that. Furthermore, I fear that if we don't take him, he'll give me the cold shoulder for months."

Jaxson nodded. "He did solve the last case, and almost single-handedly, mind you."

Jaxson was exaggerating, but without Iggy, we might never have been able to time travel back home. "Okay, we'll let him come if he gets the all-clear."

Jaxson grinned, looking as if he'd won some legal battle, even though I was the one to bring up taking Iggy. After finishing our drinks, Jaxson headed to the sheriff's department to check out the computer while I returned to the office. I'd already texted Rihanna to say she needed to see the psychic after school, because she had something important to tell my cousin. I hoped the news about needing to admit that she loved Gavin wasn't too traumatic for her, but it was the only way for her to stay safe. If for some reason she denied it, then she'd be staying home for sure—as would Gavin.

Within a half hour of my return, Rihanna came back, but she didn't meet my eye.

"How did it go with Gertrude?"

"Seriously? You know what she told me, and I'm still confused. How can being in love stop a monster?"

I was happy that admitting her love for Gavin hadn't been the impediment. "I am concerned about that, too, but Levy says that is what two different books say."

"Do you believe it?"

"I think so." I wanted to be honest with her.

She let out a sigh. "I guess that means we're going to Miami?"

"It does, assuming you want to go. No pressure."

"Of course, I do. I mean, of course *we* do. Don't worry, Gertrude spoke with Gavin to make sure he felt the same way about me. He does. I admit the conversation seemed somewhat strained, but I know what we mean to each other."

Young love at its finest. "Great. We'll drive down Saturday morning since I don't want you to miss any more school than necessary."

She waved a hand. "It's the second semester of my senior year, and I've already been accepted to junior college. Besides, we aren't really doing anything important. Figuring out who killed Gavin's dad has to take precedence. Missing a day or two isn't a big deal. Trust me."

All kids said that. "We'll see. Speaking of Gavin, where is

he?"

"With his mom. He said that when he was at the morgue, he wasn't thinking about his dad as much or his stepmother. It seems to be his safe space."

"I guess that is like when you are out taking pictures: the world seems to melt away."

Rihanna tossed me a half smile. "You're right, which reminds me that I need to do more of that—but after we track down the killer."

"Spoken like a true sleuth. Before you head into your room, I thought we might visit Hex and Bones Apothecary."

"Why?"

I told her about our conversation with Steve. "We might be safe from certain death from having our hearts turn black and hard, but this person might have an arsenal of magic bigger than one spell."

She slid down onto the sofa. "That's a scary thought. Have you ever done a spell to harm someone before?"

"No, but whatever I do, I'd like it to be temporary—such as make this person light-headed, so he passes out, enabling us to get away."

She grinned. "Or maybe you can make his muscles freeze for a minute."

"That is a good idea, but let's see what Bertha can offer. Hopefully, it's a spell she's tried before."

Rihanna stood. "I'm always up for learning something new, but why not ask Gertrude?"

I figured she'd ask that. "I really don't want her telling Levy. He might think I'm trying to usurp his power or something."

"He would never think that."

Rihanna and he were close. "I know, but I've disturbed the Poole family enough for one day. We'll have to see Bertha eventually. Her shop will have the needed ingredients to do whatever spell we choose."

"Works for me."

Chapter Eight

RIHANNA AND I entered the Hex and Bones Apothecary, and when I didn't see the owner, my heart sank. The last time Bertha went *missing*, the spell I received ended up quite different from what I expected.

"Where is she?" Rihanna asked peeking around some of the bookcases.

"Maybe Bertha's in the back." Or at least I hoped she was. A new employee, slightly older than me, was behind the counter. "Let's ask that lady."

The woman with the dark auburn hair stopped what she was doing and smiled. "May I help you?"

"I'm looking for Bertha."

"I'm afraid my grandmother is not here. Maybe I can be of assistance."

Her granddaughter? I knew about Bertha's sister but not any other relatives. "It's kind of *personal*."

I wasn't sure that was the right word, but telling her I was in love with Jaxson, and that being so would prevent me from some horrendous death would raise a lot of questions that would take too much time to answer.

Rihanna placed a hand on my arm. "Actually, my boy-friend's father was murdered a few days ago by a very powerful sorcerer. We've recently learned we are immune to one of his more deadly spells, but in case we run into him, and he has more talent than we're expecting, we'd like something to keep him occupied for a few minutes while we escape."

The woman looked between us. "Are you serious?"

Did she think because a teenager asked that she was making it up? I had enough sense not to ask that, however. "Very much so. Bertha has always been able to help me out." Her grandmother was a practicing witch, so most likely her granddaughter practiced, too. "Are you a—"

"A witch? Yes. I'm Elizabeth Murdoch."

Whoa. I introduced both of us, and we shook hands. "I normally don't ever use witchcraft to harm anyone, but this person—whose identity isn't known to us yet—could kill us, and I want to be prepared."

"Totally understandable. I take it any kind of candle lighting or potion making is out of the question since you won't have a lot of time to prepare?"

I was impressed that she grasped the situation so well. "Yes. That is why I was hoping there might be some kind of protection spell you could put on us and our boyfriends. Furthermore, it would need to last a few days since we have to travel to Miami to find this person."

"Hmm. That might be a little out of my league."

"Okay, then do you know of a spell to freeze a person so he can't move for a minute or two while we get away?"

She smiled. "I might have what you are looking for. Give me a sec."

That kind of spell actually existed? I hadn't expected that. As soon as the woman ducked into the back room, I spun to face Rihanna. "Do you think she's for real?"

"Very much so. The vibe I got from her is intense."

"Meaning she might be as powerful as Bertha?"

"Maybe more so."

How exciting. A minute later, Elizabeth motioned that we join her in the back. Rihanna and I walked around the counter and entered the storage room/office.

"I spoke with my grandmother, and she thinks very highly of you, Glinda."

"That is good to hear. I think the world of your grandmother, too. She has helped me more times than I can count." Without her, Nash might be dead, not to mention a lot of other potions she's provided me with have aided a lot of people I cared about.

Elizabeth pulled down a jar. "This contains a special powder. It will sound very strange, but a witch can only use this one time. The label is very specific about that. That means, even if you ask for more, I can't give it to you. It's like the powder has a mind of its own. It seems to know if you've used up your one chance."

How odd. "Is there some kind of artificial intelligence built into it?" I kind of felt silly even asking that.

"I don't know the details, but it sounds like that might be the case. If you try to fool it, this potion will know and use it against you, assuming your intentions aren't pure."

And if they are good? Then what? I would have asked, but I don't think Elizabeth would have known. "Once it is." That didn't mean Rihanna couldn't use it, right?

"What does this potion do exactly?" Rihanna asked.

"It stops time."

I almost laughed. That sounded ridiculous, until I recalled that we had just time traveled, so I guess anything was possible. "How long does it stop time for?"

"The bottle says about two minutes, but my grandmother hasn't tried it herself nor does she know anyone who has."

"I'll count on one minute to be safe."

"That would be a good idea," Elizabeth said.

I wanted to ask if this powder came with an expiration date, but she might not know that either.

"How does it work?" Rihanna asked.

"I place a small amount of the potion in a burlap sack that has a drawstring. If you are being chased or in dire need of help, open up the bag. The contents will know where to go. It senses evil."

"That's what I call real magic."

"I have to agree. Until my grandmother told me about it, I'd never heard of anything like it before."

"Me, neither, but it sounds perfect." Almost too perfect. As long as it only targeted the bad people, I was good with it.

She held up a finger. "I forgot to mention that a sorcerer can use it against you."

"To freeze time?"

"Yes, but there might be other consequences, so think carefully before you use it."

That scared me. "What kind of consequences?"

"I honestly don't know. Like I said, neither my grandmother or I have even known anyone to use this potion or have it used against them if it is their second time. Sorry. The bottle just says to beware."

"That is really strange." As long as it targeted evil, I was okay with it. "I'll take it."

Elizabeth rang it up. I expected to pay hundreds of dollars for it, but she only charged me twenty. I wasn't sure why it was so cheap, but I wasn't going to complain. "There is no spell, right?"

Her eyes widened. "Oh, my goodness. I can't believe I forgot that, too. Yes, there is. Wait here a minute. I'll write it down."

I should walk out of here right now, but what if what she said was true? Elizabeth could just be nervous.

A moment later, she returned. "Here it is. It's really simple. It's only four words, but don't practice them with the bag nearby. It might open up on itself. My grandmother said this stuff can be a bit fickle."

If this hadn't been Bertha's shop, I might have thought someone was playing some kind of joke on me. Thank goodness it wasn't April Fools' Day or Friday the thirteenth— not that I believe in either of those silly superstitions. If I had, I would have told her I wasn't interested. I unraveled the paper. Naturally, the words were in some foreign language.

"Do you know what these words mean?" I asked.

"Sorry, I don't."

My confidence was sinking by the minute. I had more faith in the *being-in-love* idea to protect us than this bag of time-freezing powder, but I thanked her nonetheless and left.

As soon as we stepped outside, I contemplated tossing the packet. "That was a waste," I said.

"No, it's real. Very real," Rihanna said.

I stopped and faced her. "You're buying this hocus pocus nonsense that some bag of brown powder will open up, float toward evil, and stop time?"

"Elizabeth believes it."

I loved her naïveté. "That doesn't mean it's going to work."

"I wish we could try it, but we only get one shot."

"Convenient, isn't it?" I was being cynical, and that wasn't a good trait. "Let's hope we don't have to use it."

"Yes, let's hope."

Clearly, Rihanna was siding with Elizabeth while I was tending toward not trusting her. When we returned to the office, Gavin and his mom were there talking with Jaxson.

Finding Elissa here set off warning bells. "Did something happen?"

"No," Elissa said. "Dr. Alvarez received the lab report back on the heart, and I thought you'd want to know."

"I do. What did it say?"

"It came back clean."

"Clean? The thing was black."

"I meant it had no poison, no bacteria, or anything specific to indicate that an illness killed him."

"That implies it has to be magic."

"It's the only explanation."

I sat next to Jaxson, and Rihanna slid next to Gavin. It might not be smart to discuss the misinformation I was given about this case in front of Gavin, but if someone had lied, I needed to know.

"I spoke with Betty who told me that Daniel was broke. Do you think there is any truth to that?" I asked her.

Elissa shrugged. "It's hard to believe, but like I said, Daniel and I hadn't been in contact for at least three months.

When we did talk, we only discussed Gavin. Daniel's finances never came up."

Gavin already told me he didn't believe it was true. "Betty also said your ex spoke to you on this trip, Elissa."

"I don't know why Betty would say that. He never even left me a message."

"I believe you," Rihanna said. That comment was mostly directed toward me. She must have heard something in Elissa's mind.

It was time to lay all of the cards on the table. "Jaxson and I spoke with Steve who said the Miami PD interviewed several of the people Daniel worked with. One person said that Daniel was being sued for falsifying some client's divorce papers. Do either of you know anything about this?"

"Dad told me that was a lie," Gavin said. "On our last call, he told me about it in case the rumor mill reached me. He said he had it under control."

Any father would say that in order to prevent his son from worrying. "He had *what* under control, exactly?"

"The lawsuit. He didn't falsify papers, and he could prove it."

"That's good to hear." His father was dead, and talking bad about him wouldn't help. It was also possible Daniel was being set-up.

"Why didn't you say something?" Elissa asked her son.

"Dad told me not to. I think he was embarrassed."

She huffed. "Typical."

I looked over at Jaxson, hoping he'd know how to diffuse the growing tension between those two.

"I checked out Daniel's computer at the sheriff's department. I only spent a few minutes on it, but I found quite a few websites he'd looked at regarding heart conditions. I also found a few sites about suspension, disbarment, and bankruptcy."

That implied he was worried about his health and his possible future income stream. "Maybe we need to look into that Ed guy—the one who was suing Daniel."

"I will, but I doubt he tried to harm Gavin's dad," Jaxson said. "Taking him to court would be enough, I would think."

"Gavin said something about driving down to Miami to ask questions?" Elissa asked.

She must want to change the subject, though her concern for her son's safety was understandable. "Yes, but we won't come to any harm."

"How do you know that? There's a killer on the loose. Who's to say he won't come after all of you?"

Since we needed to tell Jaxson and Gavin about our findings at the Hex and Bones Apothecary anyway, I explained about this new potion, and then I reminded her about Levy's claim that we would be protected if we stayed by each other's side. "So, you see, we'll be safe."

"This powder actually stops time?" Her brows rose as she dipped her chin. "Seriously?"

"Dr. Sanchez," Rihanna said. "Why is that any more ridiculous than a curse to stop a person from healing like what happened with Nash?"

Gavin's mom sobered. "You might be right. All you have to do is open up this small bag, and the magical potion will stop time for a few minutes? How do you know it won't stop time for you, too?"

I also had wondered about that. "Apparently, the potion knows who is good and who is evil."

Elissa held up her hands. "You're more experienced than I am about this potion stuff. I, however, need to eliminate all scientific explanations before I commit to the magical route."

"I get it."

"Just so you know, Dr. Alvarez asked me to reach out to anyone who might know about this black-heart syndrome, so I spoke with two Miami medical examiners to see if they've ever seen or heard anything like it," Dr. Sanchez said.

"That was a good idea," I said. "If this witch or warlock lives in Miami, perhaps Daniel wasn't the first person affected."

"Exactly. I'm hoping if there have been more deaths, these medical examiners might have discovered some non-magic related cause for this terrible affliction. When I hear back, I'll let you know. Magic or not, you might be able to find a connection between the victims, assuming there were more."

I had to smile. "You're becoming quite the detective!"

Elissa failed to hold in a brief smile. "Nash might be wearing off on me."

I loved it. The two of them were cute together, and I hoped they lasted. I turned to my three cohorts. "What time do you want to leave for Miami on Saturday?"

"We should probably wait until Sunday," Gavin said. "Everything will be closed on Sunday, so we'll just be wasting a day if we leave earlier."

He had a point. "I'm good with that. It will give Rihanna time to do her assignments in advance."

"Sure. No problem. I'll do my school work all day Saturday." She rolled her eyes and grunted. Poor Rihanna.

"Good, but tell your teachers you might be gone for three of four days."

A small smile escaped. "Will do." Rihanna planted her hands on her thighs. "Now for the biggest question."

"What's that?" I wished I read minds.

"What are we going to take for snacks."

We all laughed, something we sorely needed right then.

Chapter Nine

I COULDN'T REMEMBER the last time I'd been on a road trip. Years, I think. Even then, it wasn't with three people and Iggy, who, by the way, had been given the all-clear from Levy. He said the ancient book mentioned that animals were immune.

My last lengthy car trip had been with Drake—Jaxson's brother. He'd wanted company driving the couple of hours back home since his dad had taken ill. Thankfully, by the time we arrived, his father was feeling better. The return trip, needless to say, was quite festive.

Unfortunately, this Miami occasion was more somber than the trip back from the Harrison house. One other difference between the two events was that I was in the back seat with Jaxson, while Gavin and Rihanna were seated in front. We were taking Gavin's car since it was the newest and most spacious vehicle of all of our cars. He'd volunteered to drive the first leg of the journey, which was why the young folks were in front.

"Did you remember to buy any hibiscus flowers for me to snack on?" Iggy asked, jarring me out of my daydream.

I barely reacted. After so many years, I was used to him putting himself first. Clearly, I'd failed to bring him up as a responsible and caring citizen. "Of course, I did. I hope you don't mind that I have snacks for us humans, too?"

He lifted a leg. "Suit yourself. I'm going to crawl into the cargo area and go to sleep. Then I'll eat."

"You do that."

It was probably for the best. The five-and-a-half-hour trip would give us time to iron out our plan, and I didn't need to take the time to translate everything Iggy said to Gavin. "Gavin, were you able to book an appointment with Sandra tomorrow?"

He'd promised he'd speak with Morgana about calling her sister and explaining why we needed to meet with her. The two didn't see eye-to-eye, so I understood it would be hard for her to ask for a favor.

"I did. We're meeting her at ten."

I was happy Morgana had been able to get over some of her sister issues. "Good. Have you met Sandra before?"

I had no idea about Gavin's relationship with his family, other than how much he seemed to care for his mom.

"A few times, like at Dad's wedding and on one or two other occasions." The fact he didn't elaborate spoke volumes.

"I hope staying at your Dad's is okay for you." If my father had lived in a house and then died, I might not want to stay there.

"It is, and don't worry, I don't have any memories attached to that place. I only stayed there once after he and Morgana got married. It's her house."

That's right. She was the one with the family money. Gavin's stepmother was slowly slipping from near the top of the suspect list to the bottom. "Where did your dad live before he married Morgana? In the same area?"

"Yes. A couple of miles away, near where I grew up with Mom."

"Did you stay with him during the summers after the divorce?" The kid was still a teenager and deserved to have a normal life.

Rihanna turned around. "Glinda! This isn't twenty questions. You act as if Gavin is a suspect."

"Sorry." I had a tendency to be overly nosy.

"It's okay. I trust Glinda. She just wants to make sure her cousin is in good hands."

While I couldn't see what Gavin was doing in the front seat, he had removed one hand from the steering wheel and had reached out toward Rihanna.

His explanation wasn't the total reason I was asking questions, but it was as good as any. "Thank you for the trust."

"To answer your question, Glinda, after my mom moved from Miami to Witch's Cove, I divided my time between staying with her for a few weeks in the summer to going to camp in Miami. Dad worked a lot, and it seemed easier that way. He wanted me supervised—at least until I turned sixteen."

That sounded lonely. I would have asked more questions, but I sensed Rihanna didn't like it. "Do you have a key to get into the house?"

I know I sounded like a worry-wart, but I wanted everything to go smoothly.

"Yes, Morgana gave us her spare key. And don't worry, there's plenty of room for all of us to have our own bedroom."

Wow. The place was that big?

"Do you have a swimming pool?" Iggy asked, peeking his head up from his resting spot.

I thought he was asleep. I repeated Iggy's question to Gavin.

He glanced into the rear view mirror. "Yes, we do. Does he have swim trunks?"

What an odd comment. "No. Does he need a pair?"

"Probably not. I just don't want the gardener to think Iggy is some wild iguana. I hate to say it, but iguanas are considered pests where my dad lived. They've overrun the place, eating all of our flowers and shrubs. Basically, they've destroyed a lot of our landscaping. Mauricio isn't fond of them, and honestly, I can't blame him."

Iggy crawled over the back of our seat from the cargo area and sat between us. He looked up at me. "He can tell Mauricio to—"

I clamped down on his mouth. "Shh."

Only when he nodded did I release him. "Fine. How about if I wear my collar in the pool?"

I stroked his head. "Iggy will wear his collar to indicate he's not wild. Mauricio might not know that pink iguanas don't live in this part of the world. We can introduce him as my pet, even though technically he is my familiar. I doubt Mauricio would understand that concept." I didn't mention unless he happened to be a warlock.

"That sounds good," Gavin said. "Mauricio will make sure nothing happens to Iggy."

My familiar looked up at me. "Do you think I can make some friends with the wild iguanas?"

My heart broke at that question. "I'm sure you will, but

they won't be able to talk back, so I don't know how much fun that will be."

"That's okay." He turned around, crawled up the seat, and retreated to his resting spot.

We divided the driving into four segments so no one person would get tired. The rule was that the driver would be the one to choose the music. At the moment, we were listening to some horrible song that Gavin claimed was a great rap classic. Trust me, it couldn't be a classic by anyone's standard.

When it was my turn to drive, I wasn't planning on playing any golden oldies from the sixties or seventies, but come on, I wanted there to be a tune involved in the song. Most likely, I'd pick some upbeat Country hit.

In the end, it didn't matter which song Gavin or Rihanna played, because I fell asleep for the first half of the trip anyway. I had to say that Jaxson's lap made an excellent pillow. Only when we arrived at a rest stop did he finally wake me.

As soon as I got out to stretch, the air seemed really muggy, but I guess that was to be expected considering how far south we were. Because we wanted to make good time, we decided to eat the sandwiches I'd packed instead of stopping for a meal. Due to that decision, we made it to Morgana's house a little before five. It helped, too, that the Sunday traffic had been light.

When we piled out of the car, I couldn't help but whistle. "This place is amazing."

The house and grounds must have cost a fortune. It sure didn't look like Daniel Sanchez had money problems after all, though the upkeep alone would cost a lot. So what if it was Morgana's house originally? Once they married, I bet Daniel had helped pay for things.

I looked around for the gardener and any other staff, but no one seemed to be working. Either their shift didn't include weekends, or Morgana told them she planned to be away for a few days and to take the time off.

Gavin opened the front door and showed us in. The home was modern and upscale, though the black and white theme really wasn't my style. "I had no idea this place was right on the ocean."

"Yeah. Only the best for Morgana and Dad." His comment dripped with sarcasm.

I walked to the large picture window that overlooked a massive pool, a grassy area, and then the ocean. It said a lot about Gavin that he didn't seem drawn to this kind of rich lifestyle. His mom's house was small, and apparently, he didn't mind being with a girl who lived at an office.

From around the corner came a man carrying a pool skimmer. "Looks like Mauricio is here." He looked like an older version of the picture I'd seen.

Gavin looked up. "I guess I forgot to mention that he lives on the property in the cabana."

Interesting. That meant he had daily access to Daniel. While Mauricio had on jeans and a long sleeve shirt, I could definitely see his muscles. His tan skin and thick dark hair would make any woman take a second look. The question was whether or not Morgana was interested in him. Gavin's dad was descent looking but rather out of shape. Sure, Gavin's dad might have been a lawyer, but if Jaxson's research was right,

Mauricio has a medical degree, something that might appeal to her.

"What do you know about Mauricio?" I asked Gavin.

"Not much. He seems really nice. Every time I've been here, the place looks great."

"Is his English good?" Shoot. That implied I knew he'd come from someplace else.

"He has an accent, but he speaks fluent English. Why?"

"Morgana pointed a finger at him, so Jaxson did a little research."

Gavin walked over the open kitchen and retrieved four glasses. "Ignore Morgana. She and Mauricio got into a fight a while back, though I don't know over what. I think she accused him of being a suspect because she wanted to get him into trouble. He might not even be here legally."

"I thought if he had a job, he could get a Green Card."

"I wouldn't know."

I doubt Mauricio would tell us the truth if it meant he could be deported. I would consider asking him, but rushing out and grilling him now was not the way to get answers. Maybe tomorrow. And I'd make sure I had Rihanna with me.

Gavin poured us some water. "I'll show you to your rooms. Then maybe we can grab something to eat."

"That sounds great."

"I'll stay here and watch the gardener," Iggy said.

I chuckled. "You do that. Make sure he treats the other iguanas well." From the way every hedge was perfectly manicured, they certainly didn't appear to have been attacked by a hoard of hungry reptiles anytime in the near past.

I FELT A little funny dressing up in a suit, but if I wanted to be taken seriously at the law office, I figured I should look nice. My outfit was dark plum with a light cream-colored blouse.

Rihanna wore nice black slacks and a light blue blouse. Ever since she started working on her psychic skills with Gertrude, my cousin had slowly moved away from her all-black attire. I had to admit, she looked striking. I could see why Gavin was so taken by her.

As for the men, both Gavin and Jaxson wore black slacks and button-down shirts and looked like they could have worked at this law firm.

We were all seated in a waiting area when a petite blonde came out from one of the offices. "Ms. Cortez will see you now."

All four of us stood and followed her in. Sandra Cortez came around from behind her desk and hugged Gavin. "I am so sorry about your dad. He was a good man."

I held my breath, hoping Gavin wouldn't get into it with her about how his father had failed him. "Thanks."

"Please sit down."

Gavin introduced us all. We had decided to let everyone we spoke to know our agenda. I told Sandra that I was a witch who was looking for someone capable of harming another human being using magic. We wanted the sorcerer to fear we might expose him—or her. Had we not been immune, or if I didn't have the magic potion on me, that would have been quite dangerous should this witch decide to come after us. In the end, we figured it was the only way to find him.

"Tell me how I can help," Sandra said.

I was a bit surprised by her lack of response that I had some powers, but maybe she was familiar with others like me. I inhaled, ready with my tale. I only hoped Rihanna would be able to tell what Sandra was thinking.

Chapter Ten

"I'M SURE YOU know that Daniel died under strange circumstances," I said.

"My sister explained about his heart being damaged," Sandra said.

"Did Dad complain of heart problems?" Gavin asked.

Sandra shook her head. "He didn't say anything to me, but that's not surprising since we weren't close, despite being co-workers."

Jaxson pulled out his phone. "But you used to be close, didn't you?"

I didn't need my cousin to tell me Jaxson had struck a chord. I could see the shock on her face, though she tried to hide it. "Yes. We dated for a while."

That I didn't know. "What happened?" I tried to sound sympathetic, but I don't know if I pulled it off.

"Two lawyers in the same firm are bound to disagree about a case or two. It happened so many times that we decided we weren't meant for each other."

"I can understand that," I said. "When did your sister come into the picture?"

"About six months after Daniel and I broke up. She actually used our firm for her own divorce. We thought it best if I didn't handle her case, so Daniel took it, and the rest is history."

"How did that make you feel?" No, I wasn't a shrink, but sometimes the questions they asked were good ones.

"I was fine with it. As I said, we'd already broken up by then."

"You weren't jealous when they started dating?" Rihanna asked. "It would be natural. If you couldn't have him, surely your spoiled sister shouldn't have him either."

Ouch.

Sandra's mouth opened. Clearly, Rihanna had read the woman's mind. "No comment."

When her lips remained firmly pressed together, I changed the subject. "What happened to Morgana's ex-husband?" It was remotely possible he might have done away with Daniel, because he realized he'd made a mistake in divorcing his rich ex-wife.

"He's remarried. To his secretary. I've heard they are quite happy." She lifted her chin as if she knew why I'd asked.

For now, I'd cross his name off the list. One could only focus on so many people.

"Are you a witch?" I wanted to strike while she was off-balance from refusing to answer the question about being jealous.

"What? Of course not. There are no such things as witch-es."

I really wished I had the ability to levitate something so I could show her witchcraft existed. "I beg to differ. As I mentioned, I'm a witch, and Daniel died from a witch's curse—though not at my hand."

Yes, it could have been a warlock, but I didn't need to be debating semantics with her.

She laughed, but I could tell it was forced. Sandra sat up straighter and sobered. "If a witch cursed Daniel and killed him, prove it."

That was the problem. We couldn't, and telling her about my necklace glowing bright yellow when I passed it over his heart would fall on deaf ears. "The autopsy showed the heart was black and hard. I actually saw it."

"I heard about that. I will admit that is strange since he was fine a few days before he went up to Witch's Cove, but then, I'm not a doctor."

"Your instincts were spot on. A man doesn't go from fit to diseased in only a few days." Or so I believed.

"It wasn't a stroke then?"

"No. It was a curse."

"Whatever. I am busy. So, if you wouldn't mind?"

"We're almost done. What can you tell me about the man who was suing Daniel?" I asked.

"Ed Whitlow? He's a blowhard. He didn't have a case."

"Are you sure?" Gavin asked.

"Yes, I'm sure. He made it up that your dad cheated and falsified records, because he didn't want to pay his ex-wife the money she deserved."

"Was he mad enough to maybe kill Daniel?" I asked.

"Kill him? Ed Whitlow is a short, skinny man who couldn't take down a ten-year-old girl."

This woman didn't seem to understand anything about the power of witchcraft. Maybe she wasn't one after all. It also seemed as if she wasn't involved in Daniel's murder. If she had been, she would have let us think Mr. Whitlow could be guilty. "For the record, a witch or warlock doesn't need muscles to harm someone."

I was getting a bit tired of trying to prove our existence, but there was nothing I could do to show her, other than cloaking myself. That, however, required me to say a spell, which unfortunately I'd forgotten. Besides, I'd been warned about trying it too many times. Trust me, I'd felt the consequences of doing it repeatedly in the past, and I didn't like it.

"If you say so."

"Do you have his address?" Jaxson asked. "I'd like to hear Whitlow's side of the story."

I bet Gavin wouldn't appreciate hearing lies about his dad.

"Sure." She typed something into her computer, wrote down the information on a slip of paper, and handed it to him.

"Thanks."

"Can you think of anyone who *would* want to harm Daniel, present company excluded naturally?" I asked.

Sandra pressed her lips together, looking as if she was trying to come up with a suspect. "None that I can think of. No."

"Who will be the firm's new partner now that Daniel is no longer here?" I asked.

Sandra's face turned pink. "I will be. I've already been asked, and I accepted."

That seemed like motive to me, but without knowing if she was a witch, it wouldn't help. I didn't feel there was anything else to learn from her at the moment. I looked over at my three cohorts to see if they had anything to add, but none of them said a word.

"I appreciate you taking the time to talk to us." I hoped she wouldn't charge us for her time, but if she did, we would pay.

Once we were outside, Gavin suggested we go to a coffee shop he used to frequent when he lived here. That worked for me. I could use the caffeine and maybe something to eat.

I didn't ask anyone's opinion until we were seated and had ordered. I leaned back in the booth. "I'd like to hear everyone's take on what Sandra said. Who would like to go first?"

Rihanna raised her hand, and I nodded. "I think she doesn't know anything about witchcraft, but I believe she harbors quite a lot of animosity toward her former brother-in-law."

"I can't say I know Sandra all that well," Gavin said, picking up where Rihanna left off, "but I think that is true."

"Do you know why she was angry with your dad?" I asked. "Was it because she was still interested in him, or because your father was in her way when it came to getting that partner job?"

Gavin shrugged. "I really don't know. Morgana didn't say either, but I wouldn't trust my stepmother or Sandra to tell the truth."

"Good to know." I turned to Jaxson. "What's your takeaway?"

"I'd be totally guessing here, but something weird was going on when she spoke about Ed Whitlow."

"What do you mean?"

"I have no proof, but could she have paid him to sue Daniel? Perhaps she forged the papers and tried to blame it on Daniel to get him suspended."

I whistled. "That is low. I have to say it could honestly be any of those scenarios. I suppose we could speak with Ed Whitlow, but do we think he'd tell us the truth if he was in cahoots with Sandra?"

"Highly doubtful," Jaxson said. "He's not going to admit to a crime. He'd have nothing to gain and everything to lose."

"I think we should talk to Mauricio," Gavin said. "He and Morgana were chummy at one time. Maybe she told him something, off the record of course, that we could use."

I wondered what his definition of chummy was. "Sure, and if Sandra is involved in Daniel's death in any way, she'll let it slip to this person that I'm a witch. It might help draw him out."

"For all we know, the spell has already been set in motion," Jaxson said.

I shivered at that thought. "It won't do any good, thank goodness."

Jaxson clasped my hand. "Let's hope not. Will you promise to tell me the second you feel strange in any way, though?"

Now he was being overly protective. "I could, but if this love potion notion is wrong, there is nothing we can do to stop certain death."

"Don't talk like that."

I didn't want to bring the whole group down. "You're right. What do you say once we finish our meals, we go back to Morgana's house for a swim?"

"Why?" Rihanna asked.

"I want to get Mauricio to talk, and what better way than to show him we are four fun-loving people?"

Rihanna looked over at Gavin. "What do you think?" she asked.

"I'm game. I've chatted with Mauricio on several occasions, and like I've said, he's always been nice."

"When you spoke to him last night, did he think it odd that we'd come to the house so soon after your dad's passing?" I asked.

"No, I think he assumed I was there to look through some of my father's things. I didn't really say why we were there other than being at my dad's house, surrounded by his things, helped me cope with my grief."

I rubbed his shoulder. "I truly am sorry, Gavin."

"Thanks." His chin trembled.

If that had been an act—which I didn't think it was—it certainly was a convincing one.

"Did you ever mention to Mauricio that you were going to intern with your mom at her morgue?"

"I might have," Gavin said.

"Did Mauricio comment about having a medical degree?"

Gavin chuckled. "Mauricio is the gardener who also takes care of the pool."

"Yes, but we believe he was a doctor in Mexico."

"That's ridiculous."

I looked up at Jaxson. "Want to tell Gavin what you found out?"

"Sure." He told him about the article. "Are you sure he's not going to school or anything?"

Gavin said nothing for a minute. "I mean, I guess he could be. He only works at most forty-hours a week. After work he's free to do as he wishes."

"Morgana might know," I said. "Do you mind texting her?"

"I can do that."

No sooner had we entered the house when Morgana texted back. "Yes, he is doing some kind of online course," Gavin said.

"Did she say why he left Mexico?" I asked.

"Nope, but I didn't ask either."

I wasn't sure what to make of it. "I think it's time to find out about this intriguing man." I looked around. "Iggy?"

The house had been locked up, so he couldn't have gone outside.

"You called?" He was hiding under the sofa.

"How did it go?" I asked.

"You first."

Sometimes Iggy could be a pain. I lifted him up and carried him into the bedroom so I could change into my bathing suit. I gave him the short version of our conversation with Sandra.

"She dated Gavin's dad, and now he's dead? Interesting," he said.

"Are you saying there is a connection?" Sometimes Iggy could be quite intuitive.

"I'm not saying anything, and since I couldn't go outside, I couldn't find out much."

"What are you implying? That I should have let you loose, so Mauricio could have tried to capture you?" I didn't add and maybe kill him.

"It was probably better that I stayed inside. It gave me time to come up with a plan without worrying about being captured and killed by some gardener."

I tried not to smile. "A plan, huh? What kind of plan?"

"You let me out, and as soon as Mauricio goes into his cabana, I'll cloak myself and sneak in."

"That's not a bad idea. Do you want me to remove your collar?"

"Why?"

"It says Detective Iggy on it. I think that might raise suspicion should you lose your cloaking ability."

Iggy ran his claw over his collar. "I guess, but I hope Mauricio doesn't think I'm an ordinary iguana if he sees me."

"Then don't get caught." I had every confidence in Iggy.

"Okay, but don't tell Jaxson I'm not wearing it."

"Why not?"

"He gave me the collar. He might think I don't like it."

"I appreciate that you care so much." I lifted up Iggy, took off the collar, and put him back on the floor. "I need to change, so get out of here. And tell Jaxson and Rihanna your plan, so they can let you out as soon as Mauricio is out of sight."

He tilted his head. "Then Jaxson will see I'm not wearing the present he gave me."

Iggy really seemed concerned. "Fine."

I left the bedroom and made my way to the large, sliding glass doors that overlooked the pool. I opened it a nudge. "Go, but be careful."

"I will." From the way he rushed off, he was quite excited to be on another adventure.

Chapter Eleven

ONCE I WAS sure Iggy was hidden safely in the shrubs, I returned to the bedroom to change into my swimsuit. It was a bit chilly out, but Gavin assured us the pool was heated. It must be nice to live in such luxury. Or not. It actually seemed a bit lonely, but I would never have to worry about that problem.

When I returned to the living room, Gavin had a stack of beach towels ready. "What's our plan?" he asked.

I told them that Iggy was on it. "If Mauricio opens his cabana door, Iggy will cloak himself if need be and sneak in."

"He can't do computer research, can he?" Gavin asked.

I guess Rihanna never fully explained my familiar's talents. "No. That's Jaxson's department, but Iggy can tell us if there is a computer. Should Mauricio make a phone call, Iggy might be able to hear both sides of the conversation. His hearing is amazing. It's his memory that is a bit faulty."

"If Mauricio sees his collar, we might have some answering to do," Jaxson said.

"Yeah, about that." I explained that I removed Iggy's collar.

"That was smart."

Rihanna pulled open the sliding glass door. "I thought

someone suggested we go for a swim so we can show Mauricio we're here for a good time."

"True."

We all piled out of the house. True to his word, the pool was heated, and I couldn't remember the last time I went swimming when it wasn't in the Gulf of Mexico.

Since I didn't see Mauricio, I splashed Jaxson, hoping he'd make some noise and draw him out. That was a mistake. A second later, I found myself underwater. Naturally, Jaxson let me up, laughed, and then hugged me. Nice!

A door off to the side opened. It was Mauricio coming out of his cabana.

"Showtime," I whispered.

Gavin swam to the edge of the pool to greet the gardener, and Rihanna followed. Good. They needed to stay together should Mauricio be the one and only evil warlock. But from the way he smiled, he looked genuinely nice.

"I thought I heard a car pull up," Mauricio said.

"This is my girlfriend, Rihanna, the one I told you about."

"Nice to meet you." Mauricio turned his attention back to Gavin. "Did your stepmother say when she was returning? I need to discuss changing up some of the plants."

Did he really think that sounded legit? I couldn't wait to hear what Rihanna said after reading his mind. During their discussion, I looked over at the cabana. The door was closed, and I hoped Iggy had been able to sneak inside and check things out. The problem was him getting out again.

"I need to get back to work," Mauricio said.

Work? It was almost dark—or did he mean he needed to

study inside his cabana?

"Morgana has her phone. I'm sure she wouldn't mind if you called her," Gavin said.

From the way the outdoor house lights angled across his face, I couldn't get a good reading as to what he was thinking. "I might do that."

Once the gardener left, he walked to the front of the property. "Should we see what Iggy is up to?" I asked Jaxson.

He stepped over to the side of the pool and leveraged himself out in one smooth movement. "I'll get him."

"No. I need to come with you."

"If you-know-who is guilty, he has no reason to harm us. It would focus too much attention if two people who stayed at this house were affected."

Jaxson talked as if he thought the gardener was guilty. I still didn't see him as having a motive. "I want to come, but let's hear what Rihanna has to say first."

"Right."

I used the steps to get out of the pool and walked over to where Rihanna was hanging out with Gavin. "Did Mauricio think any bad thoughts?"

She sucked in a breath. "It was scary."

I squatted in front of her. "What do you mean?"

"I've never been stonewalled like that before. It was like he was able to erect an impermeable wall between our minds."

"You didn't hear anything?"

"No. I felt so…ordinary."

That would be scary. "He might be in control of his emotions. He is a doctor, after all."

She shook her head. "Gavin's mom is a doctor, and I can

tell what she's thinking."

"Rihanna?" Gavin questioned.

"But I never do."

He looked up at us. "Do you believe her?"

"Absolutely not." I chuckled. "Talk it out. We're going to rescue Iggy."

"Good luck," my cousin said.

After making sure that Mauricio was nowhere in sight, we snuck up to his cabana. I opened the door and peeked in. It was a one-room building that included a small kitchen, a two-person table, a bed, a desk, and a sofa facing a wall-mounted television.

The table was filled with books. "Do you think they are medical books?" I whispered.

"Let's see."

"What if we're caught?" I asked.

"Tell him you spotted your pet iguana going inside."

"Sounds good." I was curious if Iggy was here. He might still be cloaked. "Iggy, please come out."

A few seconds later, Iggy appeared and waddled toward me. "I'm here, but I couldn't get out."

"I figured."

"All medical books," Jaxson said.

I didn't like being in the man's private place. "I'm sorry, Iggy. Jaxson, let's go."

Jaxson was reaching for the handle when the door opened.

"What are you guys doing here?" I couldn't tell if he was angry or just confused.

I bent down and scooped up Iggy. "My pet wandered off. He has a tendency to hide."

"I was snooping," he said.

What was Iggy thinking talking out loud? *Please don't let this man be a warlock and understand what Iggy just said.*

"I'm glad you found him. What's his name?"

"Iggy."

Mauricio leaned over. "Hi there."

I squeezed Iggy, hoping he'd understand that saying anything further might put us all in danger. Thankfully, he just bobbed his head. "I think he was just hungry."

"He eats people food?"

"Sometimes, yes." Not really, but I didn't want to let anything slip.

"Come on, Glinda," Jaxson said.

"Sorry," I said to Mauricio in my sweetest voice.

When Mauricio didn't say anything more, we hightailed it out of there. I felt a little bad that I'd dripped water on his floor, but I'm sure it wasn't the first time his place got wet.

Once we returned to the pool area, I placed Iggy on the cool deck. "Don't say a word," I warned him. "Someone might be watching or listening." I smiled in case Mauricio was looking out the window.

Naturally, this guy could be totally innocent, but letting down my guard could prove disastrous.

"I think we should head inside," Rihanna said.

"Good idea. We also need to contact Dolly's cousin, Nora, to see what she's uncovered about the life of Daniel Sanchez. But first let's hear what Iggy has to say." As soon as we stepped inside the house, I grabbed a towel, dried off, and then faced him. "Anything?"

"Yes. You saw the medical books, but he also made a call."

I translated what he said.

"To Morgana?" Gavin asked. "I'd suggested he call her since he wanted to know when she was returning."

"It was a woman, that's all I know."

This was typical Iggy. He liked making us work for it. "Come on. We don't have all night."

"Okay, okay. Mauricio sounded angry. All he said was that the kid and his friends were here."

I told him what was said.

"He called me a kid?" Gavin asked.

"I know, right?" Iggy said. "Is he even old enough to be your dad?"

What was he talking about? I suppose it didn't matter. "Did you hear what the lady said?" I asked.

"She told Mauricio to forget us."

I had to think about that for a moment. I turned to Gavin. "Didn't you say that Morgana was not on great terms with Mauricio?"

"Like I said, they'd argued, but I didn't hear if they'd made up or not. It's why I think she suggested Mauricio might have wanted Dad dead."

"I hope she based her comment on more than just a grudge."

"Me, too," Gavin said.

"There's something else," Iggy said.

"What is it?" I tried to sound patient.

"I saw a picture of Morgana and Mauricio kissing."

My mind splintered into several directions. "Are you sure it was Morgana?" One of the two people might have been facing away from the camera.

"Yes. I couldn't miss the red hair. Besides, she had on that blue colored ring she still wears."

I told Gavin.

"It's a turquoise ring my dad gave her when they first started dating," Gavin said. "He told me how he had it handmade in Miami."

Oh, my. That implied she was kissing Mauricio after knowing Daniel. "Let's call Nora and see what she's found out."

"I'm coming with you," Iggy said. "There is no way I'm staying here if Mauricio understood me."

"I agree. If he understood you, it means he is a warlock. While he might be a good one, I don't want to take a chance he isn't. You'll have to stay in my purse, though."

"I know."

Iggy sounded rather dejected, but that couldn't be helped.

"I'll get ready as soon as I call Nora to set up a time and place to meet," I said.

"Can you put my collar on me first?" Iggy asked.

"Sure."

"I'll call Nora," Jaxson said. "You dress."

He always could sweet talk the women. "Thank you."

I showered and changed as fast as I could. I hoped Jaxson had been able to get a hold of Dolly's sister-in-law. As soon as I donned my pink pendant, I left the bedroom, only to find the others were waiting for me. "Did I take that long?"

Rihanna smiled. "Maybe."

"Sorry. Do we have a date with Nora?"

"We do," Jaxson said. "We are meeting her at some restaurant near downtown."

"Which means we need to hurry so as not to keep her waiting," Gavin said.

We all remained rather quiet on the ride to the restaurant. I hoped Nora hadn't uncovered too much dirt on Mauricio. That might mean we were in danger.

When we arrived, we entered en masse. "Do we know what she looks like?" I asked.

"I'm sure she'll be able to spot us. She knows there are four of us."

"Five," piped up my iguana who was inside my purse.

"Shh."

A tall, thin woman who was seated at a large table, stood, and waved to us. I was surprised the place was a seat-yourself restaurant. If this woman ran in Daniel Sanchez's circles, I would have thought we'd be eating at a more upscale establishment. In all honesty, I was glad we weren't. I felt more comfortable in a place like this. We wove our way around some tables to reach her.

"Which one of you is Gavin?" Her glance bounced between the two men.

"I am," Gavin said.

"My sympathies."

"Thanks."

"I'm Glinda, by the way, and this is my cousin, Rihanna and my boyfriend, Jaxson. I appreciate you taking the time to meet with us."

"Are you kidding? Dolly tells me all the time how much she helps solve crimes in Witch's Cove. I have to tell you, I am so jealous."

I shouldn't be surprised that Dolly bragged. "She does

help us a lot. Without her, many criminals might have gotten away."

We all sat down.

"What did you find out about Daniel Sanchez?" Jaxson asked.

Chapter Twelve

"FOR STARTERS, DANIEL'S wife, Morgana, is no saint," Nora said.

That had my attention. "How so?" I wonder if Dolly's sister-in-law had info on Morgana's relationship with Mauricio.

Nora's right eyebrow rose. "Did you know Morgana and her gardener, Mauricio Jimenez, used to date before she met Gavin's dad?"

Nailed it! Except it appeared this relationship continued even after she met Daniel. "We saw a picture in his cabana of the two of them kissing. I figured they were a couple at one point." I didn't mention that the photo was after she started to date Daniel.

"I'm not surprised it was on display. Morgana would be quite the catch for him. Are you aware that Mauricio was a doctor in Mexico and that he came to the US for asylum?"

"Was it political asylum?" Jaxson asked.

I was glad he didn't tell her that was old news. Nothing was worse to a gossip than sharing something the other person already knew.

"That I don't know."

"How did they meet?" I thought it best to change the

subject a bit, though I wasn't sure knowing the history of those two was all that important. I just liked knowing the facts—or rather the gossip.

"I have a friend who owns an upscale bar near where Morgana lives. It's a place where wealthy women feel safe visiting. Apparently, Morgana was waiting to have a few drinks with some girlfriends when Mr. Hunky showed up."

"Wasn't she seeing Daniel at the time?" I asked.

"Oh, no. She met Mauricio when she was still married to her first husband. When he started seeing someone else, she decided to retaliate."

Note to self: Morgana appears to be the vindictive type. She also seems to omit facts pertinent to the case.

I wonder where Nora learned all of this. "Do you know one of her girlfriends?"

Nora smiled. "I do. It's how I got the lowdown."

This was really good stuff. "Go on."

"Mauricio was at the bar looking lost and adorable, and Morgana saw her chance. When she learned his dilemma, she took him under her wing."

"I take it she hired him as her gardener because he needed employment to be able to stay here?" Gavin asked.

"You are a smart boy."

That, and Mauricio was a good way to get back at her husband, but I didn't need to mention that in front of Gavin.

"How long did they date?" Jaxson asked.

"They actually lived together for about a year until her divorce became final. That's when she met Gavin's dad and told Mauricio that he had to move into the cabana."

"I bet that upset him." At least he should have been upset.

"He needed the job though, right?"

"Yes. He was kind of trapped."

"Is Mauricio currently attending school or doing some training to get his medical license renewed?" Jaxson asked.

While I liked focusing on the emotional relationship, Jaxson seemed to prefer the practical aspect of things.

"I don't know the details, but he'll have to do something if he plans to practice here. I know he volunteers three days a week at the local morgue. He was a medical examiner in Mexico."

That was a great lead. "Do you know the name of the morgue and where it is located?"

"Since I figured you might ask, I did a little digging before you came. Mauricio works with a Dr. Chris Williams over on Tenth Avenue."

"That's super. And did you dig up any dirt on Sandra Cortez, Morgana's sister?" Dolly had asked Nora to research both of them. "Sandra admitted to dating Gavin's dad before her sister swept him off his feet."

The waitress came by. Finally. Thankfully, we'd already chosen our meal, so the ordering process went quickly.

"I'm vaguer on her, but she is someone to be reckoned with. She is a fiercely aggressive lawyer who goes after her opponent—within the law, of course."

"Of course," I tossed back.

"Sandra mentioned an Ed Whitlow was suing Daniel because of some papers Whitlow believed Daniel had falsified regarding the man's divorce," Jaxson said. "Do you know anything about this guy."

Nora waved a hand. "Ed and I go way back. He's an old

cheapskate who hates losing a dime even though he's richer than sin."

"Are you saying the claim against Gavin's dad might have been bogus?"

Nora held up a hand. "We lost touch over the years, but rumor has it the claim might have been a desperate attempt on Ed's part to cheat his ex-wife out of her just rewards." She turned to Gavin. "If you want a real suspect, from what I heard, it's your uncle who really hated your father."

His eyes widened. "Uncle Richie?"

"Yes, or so Daniel said."

"What did Dad say exactly?"

"When your uncle first met your mom, he threw a fit that your dad was dating her," Nora said. "He said nothing good could come from dating a woman in medical school."

Gavin chuckled. "That would have been over twenty years ago. Uncle Richie wouldn't be involved in any of this mess now, not after all these years. Besides, once Uncle Richie was arrested for breaking and entering about ten years ago, Dad kind of disowned his brother."

"Just saying. If you guys are looking for who might want to harm Daniel, I'd check him out."

We didn't need any more suspects, though I was sure Jaxson or the Miami PD could investigate him. "Thanks."

Our meal arrived, and I chowed down, not realizing how hungry I was. Even though Nora's information was wonderful and possibly helpful, I wasn't sure we gained much from our trip to Miami. Morgana had already pointed the finger at her sister and her gardener, and no one seemed to think Ed Whitlow had it in him to harm anyone. And then there was

Gavin's uncle. Had he done something recently to cause concern? We'd have to ask Steve to check with Detective Bogart, the lead on the case.

Before I could even decide who was my number one suspect, Jaxson had taken out his credit card to pay.

"No, it's on me," Nora said.

"You helped us," I said. "We should pay for your meal."

"Nonsense. I haven't had this big of a rush in a long time."

"Then thank you."

She waved to the server and then gave the girl her card. "Please give Dolly my best."

Nora seemed sweet. I don't know why Dolly appeared to dislike her. "We will."

Once we said our goodbyes, we headed back to Morgana's house. "Does anyone think we need to stay another day?" No one said a word. "Then what do you think about leaving tomorrow morning?"

"Sounds good," Rihanna said. Gavin and Jaxson agreed.

As Gavin pulled into the driveway, Mauricio was getting out of his car—a car I thought belonged to Morgana. It only now occurred to me that her car was in Witch's Cove.

This Mercedes was a high-end vehicle for a gardener, though it might have been a going away gift from Morgana for basically dumping him. If that had been the case, I imagine it would have upset Daniel, assuming he knew.

"We need to tell Mauricio we won't be staying much longer," Gavin said.

"Sounds good," Jaxson said.

The four of us piled out of the car. As we headed toward

Mauricio, Jaxson stepped in front of me and spun me around so that my back was to the gardener. Jaxson then leaned over and kissed me.

While pleasant, I wasn't sure why he did that, especially when I wanted to hear how Mauricio responded when Gavin told him about our change of plans.

Jaxson broke the kiss and pressed his lips to my ear. "Your necklace is pulsing a bright yellow," he whispered.

Every muscle in my body froze. Once I recovered somewhat, I glanced down. The pulses were there all right, but they were slowing down. I leaned back and stuffed my necklace down my shirt. Why was it doing that? I'd never seen it glow without reason. The only thing that might have caused it was that we were close to Mauricio. But why now?

I sucked in a breath once I realized I hadn't been wearing my necklace when we first met, because I'd been in my bathing suit.

"I'm good." I painted on a smile and stepped to the side.

Gavin waved goodbye to Mauricio and then motioned us inside. Clearly, he had no idea what had just happened. As soon as we were behind closed doors, I faced them.

"Mauricio is the warlock," I announced.

Rihanna looked at Gavin and then at me. "How do you know?"

"Glinda's pendant pulsed a bright yellow," Jaxson said, answering for me.

"It has never ever done anything like that before. The only time it changes color is when I'm holding it over a dead body."

"I could smell the scent of death on Mauricio. He probably just came from the morgue, despite it being pretty late," Rihanna said.

"That's not unusual," Gavin said. "People die at all hours. The cops could have asked the medical examiner to put a rush on the autopsy, and he might have called Mauricio for help."

"Are you suggesting the necklace was reacting to the smell of death?" Rihanna asked.

"I don't know."

"It never lights up when I'm at the mortuary working on a body." I wanted him to have all of the facts.

Iggy poked his head out of my purse. "I could even smell him from inside the purse."

I hadn't been paying attention. Either I was too far away from Mauricio or kissing Jaxson distracted me too much. "Are you thinking that Mauricio might have been helping autopsy a body killed with magic that somehow, what, rubbed off on him?"

"That, or his evil nature caused your necklace to pulse yellow," Jaxson said.

"Those are two very different scenarios. We can't really draw a conclusion without knowing more." Too often I'd speculate without the facts, but I was trying not to do that anymore.

"Do you think Gertrude might know?" Rihanna asked.

I had to think for a moment. "I have no idea if she would or not, but our grandmother would. It was her necklace."

"But Nana is dead," she said.

"I know, but maybe when we get back to Witch's Cove, I can contact her—with your help of course."

"Sure," my cousin said.

"Do you think we should call Levy and tell him about Mauricio?" Gavin asked.

"Not yet. We need to know for certain what the pulsing yellow means."

Before we could continue the discussion, Gavin's phone rang. "It's Nash." He sounded surprised and a bit confused. "Hey, Nash. No, I haven't spoken with her." He turned his back and walked toward the living room window.

Gavin didn't say much, but from the way his shoulders sagged, something bad had happened. I didn't dare speculate what, but since Nash had called, it might have something to do with his mother.

When Gavin disconnected, he faced us, his cheeks pale. He planted his palms over his face and bent over. Rihanna rushed over to him. "Gavin, what is it?"

It took him at least thirty seconds before he stood and faced us. "Mom's…missing."

"What?" Fear streaked through my body. Poor Gavin. First his father and now his mother? "Tell us exactly what Nash said. Maybe you misunderstood him."

Rihanna wrapped an arm around his waist and told him to sit on the sofa. Jaxson and I rushed over to the seats across from him.

Gavin swallowed hard. "Nash was very clear. He was supposed to go to dinner with Mom. When he arrived at her house to pick her up, the door was ajar. He went inside, but everything looked in place, and when Nash called her name, she didn't answer."

"Was your mom's car in the driveway?" Rihanna asked, with a very matter-of-fact tone.

"It was parked in the garage, and her purse and keys were on the kitchen table. Where could she be?" Panic ripped through his voice.

"Is Nash thinking she was kidnapped?" Jaxson asked.

"Maybe. He doesn't know, but he asked that I, or rather we, return to Witch's Cove as soon as we can."

"Then we should pack and leave right away." We had to get to the bottom of this.

Since we hadn't planned on staying long, there wasn't much to pack. We all reconvened in the living room less than fifteen minutes later.

Jaxson held out his hand to Gavin. "I'm driving."

"I can do it."

"I know, but you're worried about your mom. Besides, you need to be able to talk to Nash if he calls."

He nodded and handed over the keys.

"I take it we aren't letting Mauricio know of our second change in plans?" If he was responsible for Gavin's father's death, it was best if we didn't tangle with him.

"No, we shouldn't," Jaxson said, clearly answering for the rest of them. "We should just leave."

Without further conversation, we snuck out of the house. I would have suggested leaving on some lights so Mauricio wouldn't suspect anything, but he'd hear us drive away. The big question was what would Mauricio do once he found out we had no intention of returning?

We said little until Jaxson had reached the highway. He probably thought he was being sneaky, but I noticed him glancing in the rear view mirror several times.

"Do you think Mauricio will come after us?" I asked.

"I have no idea what he plans to do. Since we don't know if he killed Gavin's dad or not, we need to remain vigilant."

"Do you think he had anything to do with my mom's disappearance?" Gavin's voice almost cracked.

I turned around in the seat to face him. "Not personally, but if he is the warlock, maybe he feared we'd already caught onto him. Mauricio could have asked someone to take her."

"Why? What did my mom ever do to him? They've never met—as far as I know."

"It could have been a warning for us to keep our noses out of his affairs. Besides, your mom believed magic was involved. Why else would she contact her medical examiner friends if she didn't? That could have been enough to trigger her capture," I said.

"Mom consults with other MEs from time to time when she's stumped. Regardless, how did he know we'd found him out? Your necklace didn't start glowing until after we got back to the house from dinner. By then, my mom had gone missing."

"Oh. When was the last time Nash spoke with her?"

"About an hour before he went to pick her up. That would have been while we were on our way to dinner."

"You're right. The timing doesn't match. I'm sure Nash is doing everything he can to find her, but we should warn him that he needs to be careful."

"Why?" Gavin said.

"I'm not sure why I said that. Maybe there are other warlocks as powerful as Mauricio in Witch's Cove or in a neighboring town who your dad's killer contacted."

Jaxson reached out and lightly clasped my arm. "Gavin

has enough to deal with."

"You're right. Sorry." I turned back around again.

For the next hour, we kept the conversation to a minimum. Anything we could say at this point would be speculation. I snapped my fingers. "Gavin, do you know which medical examiners your mom called about whether or not they had seen another heart like your dad's?"

"No, just that they were friends of hers from Miami."

"Where did she work when she lived there?"

"At the city morgue."

My body sagged.

"What are you thinking, Glinda?" Jaxson asked.

"What if Mauricio is volunteering at the same morgue where Elissa worked? If he learned about someone asking questions about this spell, he might have freaked out—assuming he's guilty."

"Nora said Mauricio worked with a Dr. Chris Williams," Rihanna said.

"I'll call him tomorrow," Jaxson said.

Gavin's cell rang. "It's Nash…. Did you find her?… Can I put you on speaker?"

Chapter Thirteen

"I'VE NOT LOCATED your mom, but the day you left for Miami I installed security cameras around your house," Nash said. "With what happened to your dad, I wanted to take extra precautions."

"Mom said you were going to help her with that, and I really appreciate it," Gavin said.

"Did the cameras capture anything?" I asked.

"They did. In fact, I just downloaded the feed. Two men showed up at Elissa's house and knocked on the front door. As soon as she answered, one of the men pulled her outside, and the other placed a cloth over her face. She passed out quickly."

Gavin sucked in a breath. "Did you identify them?"

"Yes. They are two lowlifes from Miami, but I don't know where they are now. I've alerted the Miami PD to put a BOLO out on them."

"Could you see the type of car they were driving?" I hadn't meant to act like he wasn't competent.

"Yes, Glinda. It was a black Ford Fusion. This isn't my first rodeo, you know. Unfortunately, the license plate was out of frame."

I had no idea what that car looked like, but it didn't really matter. "Any guesses why they took Gavin's mom?"

"Not really, but she told me she spoke to a couple of her medical examiner friends in Miami. Maybe someone found out about the inquiry, and it scared him," Nash said.

It was good to know we'd drawn the same conclusion. I told him that the man we thought could be the evil warlock volunteered at a morgue in Miami. "If it is the same place, maybe he believed Elissa was getting a bit too close to the truth."

"It's a good theory, but why draw attention to the fact he's worried? Wouldn't he be better off leaving well enough alone?" Nash asked.

Gavin nodded. "It's possible Mauricio just wanted us to leave Miami after he found Glinda and Jaxson snooping in his room."

Darn. "That could be it."

Gavin then told him about my necklace glowing yellow. "I didn't see it since I was facing away from Glinda, but Mauricio could have caught sight of it. Or else he sensed it."

I hadn't thought that the warlock might have felt the pulses coming off the stone. "That's possible."

"When you get back to town, call me," Nash said. "I don't care what time it is."

It would be late, but I understood that worry kept no hours.

Jaxson drove the whole way home even though I offered to take a shift. Gavin wasn't fit to negotiate the traffic, and Rihanna needed to keep him company.

When we were close to town, Gavin spoke with Nash who said to meet him at the sheriff's office. Once we arrived, Jaxson parked in front where Nash was waiting for us. He wrapped an arm around Gavin's shoulder. "We'll find her."

Gavin dipped his head. "I know. Any news on the guys who took her?"

"Nothing new." He escorted us inside.

I turned to Rihanna. "We should try to contact Nana."

"Now?"

"Why not?" I asked. "I don't think ghosts keep regular hours."

"I'm not sure I can do it by myself. I mean, I talked to my dad a few times, but this is different. We need Gertrude."

"It's too late to disturb her."

"Ladies," Nash said. "What's going on?"

"Remember I said that my necklace glowed yellow when we returned to Morgana's house?"

"Yes, and you think it had to do with the gardener, Mauricio."

"I do." I explained again that while Mauricio might not have spotted my necklace glowing, he could have sensed it. "He might believe we know he's a warlock—like the one who killed Daniel."

"What does this have to do with this Nana person?" Nash asked.

I should have explained better. "Nana is Rihanna and my grandmother. She is the one I inherited the necklace from."

Nash's eyes widened. "I see, and you think she can tell you whether or not it means Mauricio is the warlock who used magic to kill Daniel?"

"Yes."

"Do you believe she's been chatting with Daniel, assuming they are in the same spot?"

"How would I know? Sorry. It's been a long day. Regardless of where we think spirits go, I don't believe Daniel knows anything. Curses, as you should recall, aren't always obvious."

Nash held up a hand. "You're right. I shouldn't have said anything. By all means, contact your Nana. It can't hurt. Hey, maybe she can give us a clue where the kidnappers are holding Elissa."

I inwardly smiled. "I'll ask her, though I'm not sure that's how the spirit world works." But did anyone really know the inner workings of the afterlife—other than people who were already dead?

"Do you think you can give summoning Nana a try?" I asked Rihanna.

She glanced at Gavin and then shrugged. "I guess we have nothing to lose."

"No, we don't." I rarely saw Rihanna unsure of herself. I turned to Nash. "Can we use the conference room?"

"Of course."

"You don't have any candles by chance, do you? If not, I can run across the street and get some of mine."

"Surprisingly, we do. The electricity goes off frequently enough that we began to stock them as well as flashlights."

"Great." We moved into the conference room while Nash retrieved the candles. I mentally rehearsed what I wanted to ask my grandmother. She'd appeared as a ghost once before and then just showed up twice more without me prompting her, which meant I had no idea what she'd do now. I was hoping that by having her talented granddaughter ask her to appear that she would.

We sat around the table, but it became instantly clear that

we wouldn't be able to reach each other's fingers in order to complete the loop, which was a must. "Darn it."

Nash came in with the candles, and I explained our dilemma.

"No problem. I'll clear off my desk and move all of the chairs around it. It will be cozy with the five of us, but we can fit."

"Six of us," piped up Iggy.

He'd helped in the past, so I was happy he wanted to participate this time. "Iggy will be joining us. Don't worry, he's an old pro."

"Who are you calling old?" my familiar shot back.

I didn't answer him.

Once we arranged our chairs around Nash's cleared-off desk and lit the candles, I nodded to Rihanna.

"The rules are simple," she said, sounding like a pro. "First, touch your fingertips to the person next to you, and whatever you do, don't break the contact, or the connection to the afterlife will be lost."

Everyone nodded. Well, almost everyone. Iggy was too good for that. "What's next?" I asked. We had two newbies who needed to be brought up to speed.

"If possible, refrain from asking questions unless it's highly relevant. I know what Glinda needs to know, so I'll be the one to ask Nana about it."

While the few other séances I'd done had been important—okay, the one to bring back Jaxson, Rihanna, and Iggy might have been the most important—a woman's life was at stake here.

"Close your eyes," Rihanna said.

I followed her instructions even though I wanted to see if our non-believers obliged. I hope for everyone's sake they did.

"I call upon my grandmother Amelia. We need your help, Nana." Rihanna briefly explained about the murdered man and the powerful magic that was used to take him down. "When Glinda was near the person who we believe is the bad warlock, her necklace started flashing yellow. What does it mean?"

I held my breath awaiting her answer. Knowing my grandmother, she'd make some kind of grand entrance. After waiting what seemed like an interminable time, I dared to open my eyes, hoping her ghost had appeared. Only she wasn't there.

If she wasn't coming, then I had nothing to lose by asking about Gavin's mother. "Do you know where Elissa Sanchez might be or who took her?"

Once more, I waited and waited. Just as I was about to give up, the front door to the sheriff's department opened, and we all looked up.

"Mom?"

The disbelief and pure joy in Gavin's voice caused excitement and relief to pour through me. I was sure everyone else was feeling the same emotion. They instantly shoved back their chairs and rushed to greet our missing person, clearly no longer caring that we had been in the middle of a séance. While I had no idea why Nana didn't show, I was sure she had her reasons. Or did she have something to do with finding Elissa? I wouldn't put it past the crafty witch.

When I clasped my pink diamond necklace, it was hot to the touch. "Nana?" I whispered. "Did you find Elissa and bring her here?"

A brief flicker appeared in the corner. Iggy wasn't facing in that direction, so I was sure I was the only one to see the light. I walked over to the row of chairs where Nash was leading Elissa.

Gavin's mom was dirty, seemingly disoriented, and probably really scared.

Nash knelt in front of her and clasped her hands in his. "What happened?"

She looked down at Nash and then at the rest of us. Elissa wet her lips. "I don't know."

I rushed over to the water cooler in the corner, filled up a cup, and took it over to her. "Drink this."

Elissa looked up. "Thank you."

We all pulled around our chairs in a circle. "What happened, Mom? You had us so worried."

"All I remember was answering the door to these two men. I asked what they wanted, but before I could stop them, they put a cloth that smelled like chloroform over my face. I have no idea how long I was out, but when I woke up, no one was in the room, or rather the warehouse."

"Which warehouse, Elissa?" Nash asked. "That might help us figure out who is behind all of this."

"The lights were off, so it was hard to see. But it was off State Road 21."

"How did you get here?" Nash asked.

"I walked."

I sucked in a breath. In her condition, that had to have been very hard. "Why didn't you flag someone down and ask for a ride or at the very least, ask them to call Nash?"

"I didn't trust anyone enough to stop them. I knew I couldn't put up much of a fight since I was still woozy from the chloroform."

"You were smart to be cautious." Nash looked over at Gavin. "There's probably not much more we can do tonight. Your mom is safe, and that is all that matters. Why don't you take her home? She's been through a lot."

"Nash, since we haven't found the person behind this, if a warlock is involved, Rihanna should stay at the house with Gavin. And you, too." I wasn't about to ask him if he loved Elissa. I wouldn't embarrass him like that, but his feelings for her seemed to be strong.

"Sure. That's a good idea," Nash said. "Glinda and Jaxson, why don't you escort Rihanna back to her place so she can grab a few things? I'll do the same and meet everyone back here."

"That will leave Rihanna, Gavin, and Elissa vulnerable for a few minutes. Since I doubt Elissa is up for going with us, how about Jaxson and I throw a few things in a case for Rihanna? It won't take but a sec."

Rihanna nodded. "I'm okay with that."

While Gavin and Rihanna waited with his mom, the three of us, along with Iggy, left.

"Gavin, to be safe, lock the front door," Nash said. "No telling what the goons will do if they find your mom has escaped."

"Will do."

Ten minutes later, we were back, and Nash wasn't far behind.

Now that Rihanna would be staying at Elissa's with Nash

and Gavin, I knew she'd be okay. I, however, had no intention of being by myself. For starters, I'd announced that I was a witch. Secondly, I was wearing the necklace that had pulsed yellow.

I hugged my cousin. "We'll see you tomorrow."

"You two be careful," Rihanna said. "Elissa isn't the only one who might be in danger."

"I know."

On the way out, we grabbed our suitcases from the back of Gavin's car, and then watched them help Elissa into his backseat. He took off with Nash right behind them.

Jaxson looked around. "Ready to head back to your place?"

"Yes. You're staying with me, right?"

"I wouldn't even consider letting you be by yourself. I'd suggest my place since it has two bedrooms, but my house is more isolated. Your apartment is probably safer. You do have the magic powder ready just in case, right?"

"I do."

Even though we were crossing the deserted street for the third time tonight, I kept expecting someone to jump out at us. "How is your martial arts training coming?"

Jaxson chuckled. "You don't need to worry, pink lady. I might not be able to take down more than a couple of thugs at once, but I can protect you. As soon as this case is solved though, I plan to increase my practice hours."

"You do realize that no amount of fighting skills will help if a warlock is involved."

"I know."

The moment I stepped into my apartment, my anxiety

level dropped. Jaxson locked the door behind us, and Iggy crawled out of my purse.

"That was intense," Iggy said. "Why did those guys just let Dr. Sanchez go?"

"That's an excellent question. When we catch them, we'll ask them," I said.

"Iggy," Jaxson said. "The more important question is who hired these guys and why?"

"I'm voting for Mauricio," my familiar said.

"Darn. We should have asked Elissa which medical examiner she called to find out whether there were any other hearts like Daniel's."

"And if it turns out to be Dr. Chris Williams, will that be enough evidence to point a finger at Mauricio?"

"Point a finger? Maybe. Prove anything. No."

Chapter Fourteen

THE NEXT MORNING after a very restless night of sleep, I decided to take a much-needed shower. Before I ducked into the bathroom, I listened to see if Jackson might be up, but only light snoring came from the outer room. Good. He needed his rest.

Even after tossing and turning for hours, I'd not been able to come up with a solid reason why anyone would take Dr. Sanchez if they didn't mean to harm her. And what had happened to the two men guarding her? Were they told to leave her at a warehouse? If so, why? And then there was the issue of my blinking necklace. What did it really mean? Ugh. I had so many unanswered questions.

Not wanting to keep Jackson waiting, should he need to use the only bathroom, I jumped in the shower and quickly washed.

Once done, I grabbed my pink towel from over the shower rod and dried off. After dressing, I opened the bedroom door and found him awake. His eyes might have been closed, but he was stretching and making some cute grunting sounds.

When I inadvertently made some noise, he opened his eyes and smiled. "Good morning."

"Good morning to you. Did you sleep well?"

"Not really. You?"

"No. I had too much on my mind."

"Same."

He eased off the sofa and stood. Jackson was still dressed, but he looked totally adorable with his hair all mussed.

"The shower is free," I announced.

He dragged a hand over his head. "Is that a hint?"

He was being funny. "No."

"I could use a good rinse."

"While you clean up, I'll make us some coffee."

"Sounds divine." He picked up his suitcase and entered the bedroom.

I hadn't even made it to the kitchen when he called my name. I spun around and returned to the bedroom, not imagining what he needed. I'd already set out a fresh towel for him.

"What is it?" I asked.

"Did you see this?" Jackson pointed to the steamed-up mirror.

On it was a message that read: Believe in the Magic—N. "No, I didn't. I must not have looked at it after I showered."

"Do you think N stands for Nana?"

"It has to be, but come on. She's not alive. How could she have written this?"

"Well, I didn't write it," he said.

"Clearly this had just been written. Even now, it's fading. It must be magic. After all, we summoned my grandmother last night, and while she didn't show, I saw some lights flicker in the corner just as Elissa walked into the sheriff's office."

"Do you think it was your grandmother trying to contact

you?"

"I do. She might not have shown up right away because she was out looking for Gavin's mom. And if she had been searching, it would have caused Nana to run a little late." Okay, that kind of sounded lame even to me, but it was the best explanation I could come up with.

"Let's suppose it was your grandmother who penned the message. Do you think it means that the flickering yellow light on your pendant is what you thought it meant?" Jaxson asked. "That Mauricio is the warlock we are looking for?"

"The only way to know is to ask her."

"Are you proposing another séance?" he asked.

"Possibly." My cell rang in the kitchen. "I need to get that."

I ran out of the bedroom and grabbed my cell. It was Steve. Okay, that was a surprise. "Hey."

"Glinda, can you and Jaxson come to the station now? We're assembling a task force to figure out what happened to Elissa and Daniel."

"That's a great idea. Jaxson's taking a shower, but we'll come over right after that."

That meant we'd have to grab some coffee at the sheriff's office, even though it wouldn't be nearly as good as what we could get downstairs or at the Bubbling Cauldron.

"See you in a few then," he said.

Jaxson came out of the bathroom moments later with his hair wet. "Who was that?"

"Steve." I explained about the task force. "Ready to brainstorm?"

"Absolutely."

My cute pink iguana waddled over and looked at me. "I want to come."

"I wouldn't think of leaving you behind." Who cared if half the people there couldn't understand him? I lifted Iggy and slipped him into my purse.

As soon as we entered the station, Pearl greeted us. "I heard you had quite the adventure in Miami."

The conference room, whose walls were glass, was quite full, which meant we didn't have time to give her the full lowdown. "It was interesting to say the least." I nodded to the room. "Jaxson and I seem to be the last to arrive."

She pushed a plate of cookies at me. "Take a few."

I grabbed some for the others. "You are a lifesaver."

We both entered the room, and I was totally surprised to find not only Rihanna and Gavin, Nash and Elissa, but Misty, Levy, and Camila.

Jaxson and I took the seats to the left of Levy. "Did Steve call you in?" I mumbled to my fellow sorcerer.

"He did."

Steve tapped the table. "Now that we are all here, we need to find out who this warlock is and if his agenda includes any more black-heart deaths."

Even though most of us were immune because we were with the person we loved, Levy and Camila were exposed.

"I saw something this morning," I announced.

Everyone turned toward me. "What was it?" Steve asked.

I explained about the message on the steamy glass mirror.

"How is that possible?" Rihanna asked. "I've never heard of a ghost having any kind of corporeal form."

"Me neither, but when I brushed my teeth before I showered, the mirror was clean. The only time the mirror was left unattended was when I was in the shower, and this person would have needed to get by Jaxson who was on the sofa, and then write the note, while I didn't see him—or her."

"I wasn't really asleep," he said. "I would have heard this person come in the door." He turned to Levy. "Or can some warlocks walk through walls?"

"Not that I'm aware of," Levy said.

That was a relief. Iggy crawled out of my purse and climbed onto the table. "I was up about an hour before you two sleepy heads awoke. No one came in. Trust me."

I had to translate to the few who couldn't hear him.

"Let's go with the concept that Rihanna and Glinda's grandmother managed to convey the message on the mirror. Do you think believing in the magic means that the yellow pulsing implies Mauricio is our guy?" Steve asked.

"That would be my guess." I looked around at the others. They either nodded or shrugged.

"Mauricio was last seen in Miami. Any suggestion on how we proceed?" Steve asked. "Witchcraft is not my forte."

"If my coven and I can find him, we can do a spell to take away his magic, but note: that is very dangerous," Levy said. "If he sees us, he could kill us."

I placed a hand on his arm. "You're right. It is too dangerous. You and your coven have done so much for us already. You shouldn't jeopardize your lives. We need to figure out a way to lure Mauricio here, so that your coven can stay out of sight while you guys do your spell."

Steve pulled out his yellow pad. "Any ideas how we do that exactly?"

"If he knew that Elissa was now free, would he come to Witch's Cove to take care of her himself?" I asked.

Nash shook his head. "Even if he would, I won't chance Elissa's life again. We need to find another way."

"How about asking Morgana to help us?" Gavin asked.

I hadn't thought of her. "If she called Mauricio, what would she say?"

Gavin looked over at Rihanna who shrugged, and then he dragged his gaze around the room looking for suggestions.

"Let's ask Morgana her opinion on how to get him here. She's the most familiar with him," I offered.

Jaxson clasped my hand. "I didn't think you trusted her."

"I don't, but she is our best bet. If she is innocent, she'll be a great asset. If she is in cahoots with Mauricio, we'll have to make sure someone is with her at all times so she doesn't warn him of our plan to trap him."

Nash snapped his fingers. "I'll ask Hunter to help out."

"How?" He wasn't even a deputy. "He might be a were-wolf, but I don't think we want that information to leak out beyond the people in this room."

"It doesn't have to," Nash said. "We'll ask Morgana to come to the station. Since what we are suggesting could be dangerous, we'll tell her we've hired Hunter to protect her. He can make sure she doesn't warn Mauricio."

I shook my head. "What will prevent Mauricio from killing both of them when he finds out?" We sat in silence for a bit.

"Animals are immune to Mauricio's powers," Levy said. "We could have Hunter and Morgana be at the station. We could tell Morgana there's a caged wolf in one of the holding cells who will tear Mauricio to bits if Morgana gives a particular command."

Nash chuckled. "If Mauricio shows up, how do you even know he plans to put a death spell on them? And if he tries one, do you envision Hunter running off to the cell to get this werewolf? Then, out of sight of Morgana and Mauricio, he'll strip, shift, and return?"

"Why not?" Levy said.

Steve held up a hand. "Let's keep that idea on the back burner for now. We first need to decide if we want Mauricio here. I admit it seems the safest way for Levy and his coven to strip him of his ability to destroy a person's heart without being in jeopardy themselves."

"I know what will work!" Even I surprised myself at some of my ideas. "We'll have Morgana call Mauricio. She can say that someone has been following her. She thinks it's one or two men. Being vague will be best. Morgana will have to be an excellent actress to sell herself as a damsel in distress though."

Gavin rolled his eyes. "I'll say."

"If she is innocent, she'll do anything to stay alive," I said.

He shrugged. "Agreed, and she is a survivor."

"Next, Morgana will beg Mauricio to drive up here to protect her. She could even say she heard about Elissa being kidnapped and didn't want the same thing happening to her. If Mauricio asks her how she heard about that, Morgana can say you, Nash, caught the kidnapping on camera."

"We'll have to hide Elissa someplace very safe then," Nash said.

"She can stay at my parents' funeral home. Mauricio won't think to look there."

"That's a good idea."

"You do realize your plan will take at least six hours to execute?" Steve threw in. "Miami is a long drive away."

"I know. We just drove it, but that's okay. We'll need every minute for the second part of the plan."

"The second part of the plan?" the sheriff asked.

"Yes. I have an idea, but let's see if Morgana will go for the first part before I lay out the rest. Gavin, do you want to call and ask her to meet you here?"

"Not particularly," he said without hesitation.

"I'll call," Steve said. "I'm running the investigation from the Witch's Cove end. I think she'll come in, whether she is guilty or not."

"Good."

Steve sounded very professional when he asked Morgana to join us, though he didn't give her much choice. He disconnected and faced us. "In case she is in cahoots with Mauricio, we'll tell her as little as possible."

That worked for me.

It wasn't long before Morgana arrived. She looked around and froze. "What is everyone doing here?"

Steve explained our plan—or at least a watered-down version of it.

"You want me to convince Mauricio to come here so he can protect me from the two men who I believe kidnapped Elissa?"

"You were both Daniel's former wives. Maybe there is a connection." I shrugged. "Can you think of something better?"

"No, but why are you eager to have him here at all?"

We had to tell her something. "We think, or rather I think, he might have killed Daniel. Even you thought that, remember?"

She nodded. "Okay. But why have him come here? He could harm someone else."

"We're hoping Levy, Camila, and some other coven members will be able to perform a magical spell that will prevent Mauricio from doing just that—ever again." I inhaled. "That would require us to lure him to a room at the Magic Wand Hotel. We'll say it's your room, only Jaxson and I will be there instead. That's when Levy and his group will do their magic."

So much for only sharing a watered-down version of the plan. That was the whole plan!

Morgana just stared at me. "You're serious, aren't you?"

"What part is so hard to believe?"

"The part about the spell."

I relaxed. "If spells don't exist, then there is no harm in putting one on him."

"I guess I'm good with that. Where will I be?"

"Here," Steve said. "We don't want Mauricio to retaliate in any way. I'll ask a bodyguard to be with you the whole time."

"If, and that is a big if, Mauricio believes that I'm in dire straits, I don't think he'll drop everything and drive the five plus hours up here."

"Tell him you'll pay him—handsomely," Jaxson said. "He's a gardener. He probably could use the money."

"You're right about that," she mumbled.

"I think you hold more sway over him than you think,

Morgana. I'm sure you can sweet talk him into coming. Lie if need be. Say you're devastated over the loss of Daniel, and you need Mauricio for emotional support."

She rolled her eyes at me. "Fine. I'll figure something out."

She pulled out her phone, but Steve held out his hand. "Give me a minute before you call."

Morgana's brows rose. "Because?"

"I want to make sure we can set up a room at the Magic Wand Hotel. I'll need to be able to tell you the room number."

"Ah, yes, that makes sense."

Steve left to make the call. Now that this was actually going to go down, my nerves returned.

Chapter Fifteen

ONCE STEVE SAID he'd set things up with the hotel, and Morgana made her call, Jaxson, Iggy, and I, along with Rihanna and Gavin, went across the street to the Spellbound diner to grab some lunch. Elissa and Nash said they'd keep Morgana company and order something from the Bubbling Cauldron next door.

On the walk over, we decided that Morgana should be given some kind of acting award. She'd been able to convince Mauricio to drive up to Witch's Cove pronto. Of course, the thousand-dollar bonus might have been what persuaded him. I wasn't sure if that made him a good guy or a bad one.

Regardless, even in a court of all witches, it would be impossible to prove Mauricio had been the one who killed Daniel without some proof. Having his powers stripped might be the only punishment he'd ever receive. And I was good with that—or as good as I could be.

The diner was rather empty, enabling us to grab our usual booth. I waved to Dolly who grinned and rushed over.

"I heard you guys were back. How did it go?" Her expression instantly changed from total elation to one of being serious. "And Nora. How was she?"

I smiled. "She was great."

"You don't know her then."

I was dying to know why Dolly was so against her. "What did she do that was so wrong?"

Since there was no more room in our booth for Dolly to sit, she squatted down in the aisle. "Nora is not a nice person. Did she happen to mention Daniel's brother, Richie?" Dolly rolled her eyes.

"Yes," I said.

"I figured she would. With Gavin being there, she'd not skip the chance to bash the man."

I sucked in a breath. "She mentioned she thinks he might have harmed Daniel."

Dolly shook her head. "The woman will never give it up. Before she married my brother, she and Richie dated."

"Okay, but there's nothing wrong with that." I was quite sure Dolly never left Witch's Cove, which meant she probably never met Daniel's brother.

"Normally no, but Nora maligned Richie after he dumped her. She'll say anything to get back at him even after all these years. It's just plain wrong."

It was hard to believe that sweet Nora would do that. "Accusing a person of murder is a lot more serious than getting a bit of revenge for him breaking up with her."

"Finally, you see why I don't like her."

That shed some light on things. "Thank you for that. Any help in eliminating a suspect is always welcome."

Dolly stood and grinned. She acted as if she'd won a big prize. "What can I get you guys?"

Since it appeared as if Dolly knew nothing more, we placed our order.

As soon as she left, I turned to the other three—or four if I counted Iggy. I focused on Gavin since we were talking about his dad's brother. "Thoughts?"

Gavin shrugged. "I never believed Uncle Richie would hurt Dad. I do remember my uncle mentioning some crazy lady who wouldn't leave him alone. I was pretty young and didn't pay a lot of attention, but it could have been Nora."

"Good to know."

"Fill us in on the details of this sting operation, Glinda," Rihanna said.

Iggy popped his head out of my bag. "What's my role?"

Whoops. I hadn't planned on using Iggy, but maybe he could come up with an idea on how to help.

"It's not too complicated. Morgana has already set the trap. Mauricio will show up at her hotel room—or to the one Steve just booked. Jaxson and I will be there instead. Surprise!"

"What makes you think he won't realize it's a trap and turn around?"

"Besides having Morgana move her clothes into that room to make it look legit, Steve and Misty will be in uniform in the hallway, pretending to be general hotel security. Mauricio might even think they're there to protect Morgana."

Jaxson nodded. "If I'm a warlock and had harmed a few people, it would be safer to stay in the room with two crazy kids than be questioned by the law, even if they are just hotel employees."

"We're kids?" I kind of liked that.

"To Mauricio you might be."

"Go on, Glinda," Rihanna said.

"As soon as Mauricio is in the room, Steve will signal Levy, who will be in the adjoining room with Hunter and a few of his coven members. If Mauricio tries to leave, I'll toss the magic powder at him. That will give Levy and his crew a minute or two to do the spell."

"That is quite brilliant," Gavin said.

"Thank you."

A server arrived with our drinks. "Thanks."

"Your food will be up shortly."

It couldn't come soon enough. I sipped my tea, and the drink tasted better than usual, but I might be comparing it to what we had in Miami.

"We need to think of what could go wrong," Gavin said. "And please use Rihanna and me. We can help."

That was what I wanted to avoid. "If Mauricio is powerful enough to turn hearts black, who's to say he can't do a host of other things? You might not be safe."

"Which is why you have the powdered potion," Rihanna said.

"Exactly. If he chants even one word, I'm putting him in freeze mode."

Rihanna looked over at Gavin. "We'd still like to do something."

"As soon as we eat, let's head back to the sheriff's department. I bet he and Nash, along with maybe Morgana, have thought of something."

"Sounds good," Rihanna said.

The food arrived, and for the most part, we ate in silence. I ran through all the things that could go wrong, but I failed to come up with any ideas that really concerned me.

We paid and headed back across the street. When we walked inside, the group, including Hunter, were in the conference room.

After we joined them, Steve looked up. "Ready for the big sting?" he asked.

"I hope so."

All during lunch, something had been nagging at me. "Morgana, I noticed that Mauricio drives a rather new Mercedes. Where did he get it?"

"He bought it not long ago, but you know, I didn't even ask him about it. It kind of looks like my sister's old car."

Rihanna subtly nodded that Morgana was telling the truth. I wonder why her curiosity didn't get the best of her?

I would ask Steve to run a history on the car, assuming he could do that. If Mauricio had recently acquired his car from Sandra, that might implicate her somehow. Then again, she really might have wanted to sell her car and was willing to give him a good deal.

Before I could ask Morgana anything else, Nash came into the room carrying a box. "I have the coms. I want Glinda and Jaxson to also wear a wire. We'll be listening and recording everything Mauricio says."

"You can't use that in court though, can you?" Jaxson asked.

"Not in a regular court, no, but if Mauricio admits to any kind of guilt, we'll deal with him in another way."

Since he lived in Miami, I bet the detectives there would say differently.

"What time should we be at the room?" I asked.

"Morgana," Steve said. "How about texting Mauricio and

asking him about his expected time of arrival?"

"Sure. He's a fast driver, so it might be sooner rather than later. He won't stop for anything."

Morgana did as Steve asked. "You can look at the text before I send it if you don't trust me."

Steve glanced at it. "Looks good."

While we waited for Mauricio to return the text, my nerves continued to build.

Jaxson leaned over and whispered in my ear, "Glinda, you have that tic above your eye again."

I inhaled and rubbed the offending area. "I'll be fine. I have the potion, and I have you with me. I'm good."

"Remember that Hunter will be next door ready to eat the guy should Mauricio try anything."

The fact he would be in his werewolf form calmed me. "And Steve and Misty will be able to hear our entire conversation. That's good. And I know bullets can kill a warlock."

"Yes." Jaxson gave me a half smile.

Morgana's phone pinged. "His ETA is in three hours."

Steve planted his palms on the table. "Does everyone know what they are to do?"

We all nodded.

"Just so you all know," Elissa said, "I'm still waiting to hear back from Chris Williams about whether he had other cases in Miami similar to Daniel's."

At the moment, I wasn't sure if it would matter. "Did you ask if Mauricio worked with him?"

"I didn't know I was supposed to, but I'll do that now."

"Thank you."

Steve nodded to us. "In light of Mauricio's arrival, you and Jaxson should get to the room by 3:30PM."

"Can do."

The next two hours were sure to be nail-biting ones.

"CAN YOU HEAR me?" That was Steve's voice coming in loud and clear through my com.

"I can."

Misty must have then asked Jaxson the same question, because Jaxson said he could hear her, too.

I grabbed Jaxson's hand and squeezed. "This is it."

"You're fretting again. We're going to be fine."

He leaned over and adjusted my pink pendant that probably didn't need to be moved. Jaxson just wanted me to believe that everything would go as planned.

"What if Mauricio sees us, realizes he's been had, and immediately attacks?" The chances of that were probably slim, but when I was nervous, I often made up outlandish stories in my head.

"Not to worry. I can take him down. Besides, we have two cops in the hallway and a snarling wolf in the next room."

His repeated reminder made me feel better. "Okay. Are we all set with what we're going to tell Mauricio when he asks where Morgana is?"

"If you are, then yes. You're the witch. He'll want to talk to you."

"No pressure."

"Glinda," Steve said in a soft voice. "Showtime."

Jaxson let go of my hand. "We can do this."

A few seconds later, a knock sounded on the door. "Morgana, it's me."

I inhaled and pulled it open. "Come in, Mauricio."

Thankfully, he did, though he looked genuinely confused. "Where's Morgana?"

"She's not here." I knew that was obvious, but I wanted to stall. I needed my heart to slow down a bit.

"Where is she?"

"She called and said she thought she saw someone in the lobby—someone who had followed her. Morgana asked that we come here and let you know."

"Did Morgana say where she planned to hide, or if she was coming back anytime soon?" He sounded concerned. "She called me in Miami and said she feared for her life. Now she's gone?"

"Yes. I wish I knew more."

He turned around. "I need to find her."

"Do you want us to help you look? We know the town better than you." I had no idea why I was even suggesting that. We had no intention of leaving this room.

"Sure." Mauricio nodded to my necklace that was flashing up a yellow storm. "Why is the gem in your necklace doing that again?"

Again? That meant he had felt its power when we had been at Morgana's house. This proved to me he was a warlock. Too bad the pink gem couldn't tell me if he was the one who had put the killing spell on Daniel.

Mauricio swiped the back of his hand across his forehead, acting as if my magic pendant was creating heat.

"It does that when I'm in the presence of a warlock."

"A warlock? You have to be kidding."

I looked over at Jaxson, who took a step forward. "We know who and what you are."

Mauricio shrugged. "Fine. I am one. So what? Glinda's a witch, which means we're alike."

How did he know I was a witch? Had Sandra told him? If so, when? And why didn't he deny being a warlock for a little bit longer? He sure gave up rather quickly—almost too quickly. Or he was merely calling our bluff?

Two could play at this game. "We're hardly alike. I don't harm people." I stood taller. Somehow that gave me more confidence. "Tell me, Mauricio, why did you put a curse on Daniel Sanchez that killed him?"

Mauricio huffed out a laugh. "What in the world are you talking about? I did no such thing. Why would I?"

"Let me count the ways." I wasn't sure why I said that, but now that I had, I needed to come up with a few reasons why he'd kill Daniel Sanchez. "Maybe you were angry at him because he stole Morgana, the love of your life." And no, I had little basis for that comment other than he and Morgana had lived together for a year.

"No way. I'll admit that what Morgana and I had before was good. Real good, but when it ended, it was over. For the record, I was the one who said I needed to concentrate on getting my medical license and didn't have time for a woman, especially one who wanted to be entertained all the time."

For a few seconds, I doubted myself. How did he know we were even aware he had a medical degree? I hope he assumed Morgana had told us at some point. The problem was that if Mauricio hadn't killed Daniel, would my necklace be going crazy? Would Nana have told me to believe in the magic if it wasn't accurate?

"Then did Sandra hire you to kill Daniel?"

"Sandra? As in Morgana's sister?"

How many Sandras were there? I suppose in his circle of friends, maybe a lot. "Yes, her sister."

"Why would she do that?"

The man had an answer for everything—or rather a question for every one of mine. "Oh, I don't know. Maybe because Daniel Sanchez was made partner in their law firm, and she wasn't? With him out of the way, she'd be appointed."

"I have no idea if promotions work that way. You'd have to ask her. She might have hired someone to kill Daniel, but she didn't hire me."

"Then did Morgana put you up to it?" I asked. "She might have realized that her marriage had been a mistake. After all, she was the one with the money."

Mauricio laughed at us, and I had to say the man was convincing. "Are you crazy? She loved her husband. End of story."

I was sinking fast. Could he really be innocent in all of this? Levy was a warlock, but my necklace never flashed when I was near him. "Tell me this. Where did you get the money to buy that fancy car you drive?"

While he might be able to cloak his thoughts from Rihanna, this time his face said it all. He'd been caught. "I bought it with the money I earned from being a gardener. If you didn't know, I get to live for free in the cabana."

"It's still a lot of money."

"It normally would be, but this particular car kept stalling for its owner, and since I'm quite a good mechanic, I was able to fix it. I got a great deal."

"You were a doctor and a mechanic? Aren't you the jack of all trades, Mr. Jimenez?" I refused to give him the respect of calling him Dr. Jimenez.

"What can I say? When you live in Mexico, you have to be able to do many things."

That sounded plausible. "Why wouldn't the owner spend a little money to fix it himself and then sell it at a higher price?"

"That I don't know."

"Who did you buy it from?" I asked.

"Morgana's sister, Sandra. She wanted a newer model, so Morgana put the deal together."

Aha! Either he was lying, or Morgana was. The question was, which one was it?

Chapter Sixteen

CLEARLY, EITHER MORGANA or Mauricio wasn't telling the truth. I couldn't help but wonder if Mauricio's Mercedes had been a payoff for killing Daniel. Too bad no one would ever be able to prove it was anything but what it looked like—the sale of a car. No matter what I asked, I doubted Mauricio would tell the truth. It could have been that he suspected he was being recorded, or it could mean he really was innocent.

From the way he was shifting his weight and how his gaze was bouncing around the room, he was losing patience. It was time for Levy and his coven to do their magic. Even though this was my one shot at freezing time for life, I had to trust my gut instinct that Mauricio was guilty.

I opened the bag and said, "Uruth, Sagamos, Braci, Fortunitus." I held my breath that I hadn't messed up the words. I also held my breath to prevent any of the potion from getting into me! If he wasn't an evil warlock, the power would hopefully cause no harm.

The dark brown powder floated straight toward Mauricio. Yes, he was guilty! He batted it away, but to no avail, as it entered through his nose and mouth.

He coughed, and his eyes watered. "What is that stuff?"

"It is an evil-seeker." At the moment, I couldn't think of anything else to call it.

"No! It can't be. You have to get it away from me." Mauricio kept swinging his arms—or at least he tried to—but after two or three attempts, he froze.

Oh, my goodness. It worked. The spell actually worked!! I just stood there, staring at the statue-like man. Thankfully, Jaxson was a quick thinker. He instantly called Steve and told him it was a go.

I then snapped out of my shock. I rushed to the adjoining door and yanked it open. "He's ready."

Levy and his group of four only had about a minute to perform the ceremony that would rid Mauricio of his ability to kill people by turning their hearts to near stone.

Within seconds, they'd circled their prey and lit the candles.

"You two need to leave. Your presence might interfere with the spell," Levy said.

No way I wanted to go, but there wasn't any time to argue. As quickly as we could, Jaxson and I left. I figured, we didn't have long to wait—a minute at the most.

"You both have to head back to my office," Steve said. "We don't need Mauricio seeing you out here."

I guess it would be hard to explain how we could be standing in front of him one minute and were in the hallway the next. Jaxson wrapped an arm around my waist and escorted me to the stairwell. He probably figured the elevator might not arrive in time.

We said nothing until we were outside. Thankfully, the fresh air revived me.

"That was almost scary how well that worked," Jaxson said.

"I know. It was like the powder knew who to go after. I'll have to thank Bertha the next time I see her."

"Let's hope Levy and his coven are as successful."

"The question is how will we know if it worked? Not that I don't love being with you twenty-four seven, but it would be nice to have proof that Mauricio can't harm anyone."

"We'll figure something out," he said.

"That's why we need to work on part two of the plan."

"I thought you'd figured that out."

"Only some of it."

Jaxson nodded and chuckled. "That's my girl."

When we reached the sheriff's office, Nash was with Elissa in the conference room, along with Gavin and Rihanna. Morgana was sitting by herself across from them looking rather lost, and I felt sorry for her. Nash waved us in.

As soon as we stepped inside, we were instantly bombarded with questions. We pulled out two chairs, ready to begin. "For starters, I think everything worked." I explained how Mauricio denied any involvement in Daniel's death.

"He'd never admit to anything," Morgana said. "The moment he found out I wasn't there, he probably assumed it was a trap."

That might explain his evasive answers. "He did say one curious thing."

"What's that?" Morgana asked.

"That you helped arrange for the sale of the Mercedes between Sandra and him."

Her eyes went wide and then narrowed. "That little

snake."

I had to assume that meant he lied. "Why would he tell me that you knew about the car?"

Morgana leaned back in her chair. "You know, I always had the sense that he fancied my sister." Morgana admitted that she basically stole Daniel away from Sandra.

"Interesting." That wasn't quite what Sandra said. She had broken up with Daniel long before Morgana came into the picture, but now might not be the best time to talk about that discrepancy.

"I wouldn't be surprised if my sister decided to turn the tables on me and try to take Mauricio away from me. If they ended up an item, he'd say anything to protect her."

"I thought you two broke up after you met Daniel. That meant Mauricio was fair game."

"That's true, but I didn't leave Mauricio until I was sure that Daniel and I were meant for each other. I really don't know when—or if—he and Sandra got together."

I decided not to bring up the photo Iggy saw in Mauricio's room. It shouldn't have surprised me that my familiar chose that moment to crawl onto the table.

"Something doesn't add up," he said.

Only Jaxson and Rihanna could hear Iggy—or so I believed. "What is that?"

Morgana shot a gaze over to Iggy. "Did you just talk to your pet?"

"He's not a pet, but yes. And he can talk back, but only witches can hear him."

"Oh."

I looked down at Iggy. "Go on."

"Ask about the photo. The timing is off."

I wasn't quite sure what he meant, but I turned to Morgana and asked her about it. "There was a photo of you and Mauricio in his cabana. You two were kissing."

"And you were wearing the ring Dad gave you," Gavin threw in before she could answer.

Darn. I was hoping to keep that tidbit out of it.

Morgana's face heated. "Your dad and I were at a party, and Mauricio happened to be there. I can't remember why or who'd invited him. When I was alone, he came up and kissed me. It meant nothing. At least to me."

"Who took the picture?"

"Good question. He probably paid someone to snap it so he could use it as blackmail if need be."

"Nice guy." Or not. He was brave—or stupid—to have a photo of Morgana and him in his cabana where Daniel might see it. Hopefully, he put it there after Daniel had died. Right now, I wasn't sure who to believe, but we had more important things to deal with. "What are the odds that Mauricio is in his car at this moment driving back to Miami? I'm betting he'll want nothing to do with Witch's Cove after what just happened."

"If that happens," Jaxson said, "we may never know if the spell was successful."

Nash shook his head. "He probably is unaware you stopped time, so he has no reason to rush home. But if he figures it out, we have no legal right to detain him, and I bet he knows that."

"You don't think he'll go looking for Morgana?" Rihanna asked. "He believes she left the hotel because someone was following her."

I turned back to her. "What do you think? How much does Mauricio care about you? You are his employer, and he needs you to stay alive so that he can remain in the States." Or so I believed.

She blew out a breath. "I hope you're right. There was a time when I thought he loved me, but when I met Daniel, I told him we had to stop seeing each other."

Clearly, she didn't love Mauricio then. I thought it best not to say that either or comment that what she said didn't match what Mauricio told us. The lies were mounting, only I didn't know from which side.

Morgana's cell rang, and she picked it up to check the screen. "It's Mauricio."

"Don't answer it," Nash said.

She set it down. "I'll have to at some point."

For a while now, I'd been thinking about how to get Mauricio to slip up. "I have an idea. At the moment, Mauricio probably doesn't know that his power to kill is gone— assuming Levy and his coven did their job."

Everyone turned. My ideas have always been out there, but they'd mostly worked in the past, more or less like I'd planned.

"Tell us what you're thinking," Jaxson said in a very reassuring voice.

"My plan depends on whether Morgana can sound like Sandra over the phone."

She almost laughed. "Are you kidding? We used to prank a lot of people by pretending to be each other. What do you need? I'm in. Mauricio's lies have to stop."

From her enthusiasm, this woman had nothing to do with her husband's death. "For starters, call Mauricio and tell him you're Sandra."

"I can do that, but what would I say?"

"We need Mauricio to believe that your sister drove up to Witch's Cove to arrange your kidnapping. He knows Elissa was taken. Why not you too?"

"Why would Sandra kidnap me?"

Why indeed? I looked around. "Any ideas?"

"With Daniel gone, maybe Sandra is convinced that her sister plans to win back Mauricio. Sandra then decides that she can't let that happen," Rihanna said.

My little cousin had a devious mind. "I like it."

"Playing the devil's advocate," Morgana said. "Why wouldn't my sister just hire two thugs to murder me?"

"A warlock's kill leaves no trail. That's why she'll need to ask Mauricio in person to take you out like he did Daniel."

Morgana's eyes lit up. "Oh, I see the plan coming together. How does this work exactly?"

"You, pretending to be Sandra, will ask Mauricio to meet you at the Water's Edge Motel, where you will then say that you have Morgana held captive, and that the two of you are in room 4. Tell him the motel is some dive at the south end of town on the west side, and that he can't miss it."

She held up a hand. "The only flaw is that Sandra might not have been involved in Daniel's death, which means Mauricio will know she's lying. That will put her, or rather me, in danger."

"We'll make sure nothing happens to you," Nash said.

"I'm not sure I want to tempt fate like that."

I could almost see my plan crumble right before my eyes. "I thought you were on board."

"I am, but this is plain crazy."

"Don't worry, Morgana," Nash said. "He can't harden your heart. Glinda and her other witchy friends took care of that."

Nash delivered that speech with a lot of conviction, and I hoped he was right.

Morgana's jaw clenched. "Unless he's in love with Sandra, he'd never go along with this plan. He cares for me too much—or at least he used to."

Then why tell lies about her now? "We need something to lure him with. Something that would transcend his affection for you."

"I bet Mauricio could use more money," Jaxson said. "A lot of it."

"I like it. What if Sandra tells him that once Morgana is dead, Sandra will inherit the house. When she does, she'll sell it and give half of the money to Mauricio."

Morgana sat up straighter. "Heck, I might kill someone for that amount of money." She looked around. "Only kidding. And for the record, Sandra will not inherit the house. Neither Mauricio nor Sandra know that though."

I wasn't about to ask who she did leave it to. "Then are you willing to call him and be convincing?"

Morgana blew out a breath and nodded. "Yes, but what happens when he comes into the room and finds Sandra isn't there? Or worse, calls my sister to ask her a question?"

I forgot about that. I really need to think these things through. "Let's hope he doesn't, but if he knows he's been set up, he might come anyway to take you out. Either way, we'll win."

"Glinda's right. You'll be safe. Steve will tie you up," Nash said. "When Mauricio frees you, you can beg for your life. Tell him that Sandra left for a few minutes, but that she'd be back soon."

"Assuming he doesn't just kill me." She waved a hand. "I know you won't let that happen. What if he tells me Sandra is unaware of this plan?"

I blew out a breath. "Let's hope he and Sandra don't communicate."

"Fine, but how will I know if he tries to do this spell on me? Will he have to say a chant or something first?"

She was nervous about this, and I couldn't blame her. I pulled out my phone. "Levy will know the answer to that. Hold on." I called, asked him about the spell, and then put my cell on speaker.

"The book says the spell Mauricio would use is a short one—a few words at most—but it must be accompanied by a series of fairly intricate hand signals. I think the ancient witches who created this spell didn't want it getting into the wrong hands, so to speak."

"I can see why. So, we'll know he is attempting to kill Morgana if he starts waving his hands?" I asked.

"Yes. Why do you need to know?" Levy asked. "Mauricio is now harmless."

"If we see him do some hand signals, we'll know he's trying to evoke the spell, and we can catch him. I'm assuming he has no idea his powers are gone?"

"He won't until he tries to kill someone again."

After chatting briefly, we disconnected. Nash then outlined that he and Hunter would be in the adjoining room, assuming this rundown motel had a door connecting the two rooms. Thankfully, he didn't mention his ability to shift into a werewolf and tear a person limb from limb.

Just then Steve, Misty, and Hunter came into the conference room. Nash looked up at them. "We're working on a plan for Mauricio to incriminate himself."

All three claimed the remaining seats. "Fill us in."

Nash told him the plan. "We'll need to plant a camera in the room so we can make sure Mauricio's hands remain still."

"That's easy. Glinda, if you want to watch in real time, all you need to do is download an app on your phone so that our two phones can communicate."

"I can do that."

He showed me what to download and how to use the app. It seemed simple enough.

"Misty, Morgana, Hunter, and I will head over to the motel to make sure the place has two rooms next to each other. When we're set up, we'll have Morgana, pretending to be Sandra, call Mauricio." Steve looked around. "Great plan, people."

I had to smile. "I just hope Mauricio isn't on his way back to Miami already."

"He's not. I saw him go into Dolly's."

Oh, no. "I'll text her and tell her not to engage in any conversation with him. I love Dolly, but she can't be trusted."

Steve nodded. "You do that." He turned to Morgana. "You need to come with us. We'll have to make your kidnapping look real."

"Oh, great."

"Besides watching, is there any way we can hear what's going on?" I'd already removed my com. Even if I hadn't, I don't think they'd extend very far.

"Yes. The camera will have audio. When I'm done setting it up, I'll call you, Glinda. There won't be anything to hear until after Mauricio shows up, but it will be recording the whole time."

"Okay, thanks." I hope he had a lot of minutes on his phone plan or it could cost the city a lot of money.

Chapter Seventeen

ONCE STEVE, HUNTER, Misty, and Morgana left to set up the motel room sting, I turned to Elissa. "Have you given any more thought about who might have orchestrated your capture?"

"No, but if Mauricio worked as a medical examiner, he could have learned of my inquiry and worried someone would tie him to the deaths, assuming there are more than one. He might have hired those men."

That made sense. "Then why leave you alive?"

"I have no idea."

"Personally, I think Mauricio is more afraid of you than he is of my mom," Gavin said. "You are a witch, after all."

That would imply Mauricio might not have been behind Elissa's capture. "Why? My necklace didn't pulse until after your mom had been taken."

"I know, but we had already told Sandra you are a witch, and that we were there to find the person who killed my dad."

"You might be right. Sandra might have called Mauricio and told him to be leery of me. Let's hope Levy is as good as we think he is, and Mauricio can never harm anyone again."

Rihanna smiled. "Trust me. He is that good."

While we waited for Steve to contact us, Elissa left another message for Dr. Chris Williams about whether Mauricio worked for him. She said the information was time sensitive and to get back to her as soon as he could.

In the meantime, I grabbed more coffee since the next hour was going to be nerve-wracking. I really wished we could have heard Morgana's phone call to Mauricio in real time, but she needed to be situated in the motel before she contacted him. Having the right room number was equally important.

When my cell finally rang, my heart lurched. The caller ID said it was Steve. "I'm here." I kept my voice low, though I doubt it mattered. Mauricio wasn't there yet.

"We're at the hotel room now. Click on the app you downloaded, and you will see an image."

I tested it. "It works."

"Great."

"I assume Morgana playing Sandra, called Mauricio, and he's coming?"

"Of course, and he seemed to believe her. Since he should be here any moment, we need to get in position as soon as I hide the phone. Talk later."

"Okay." Some scratching noises and a bit of static came across the line. Steve's chest appeared for a second. Then I could see him hiding the phone behind what looked like the coffee maker.

"Good luck, Morgana. Thanks for doing this." That was Steve's voice. Unfortunately, it was a bit muffled.

A door opened and closed, and then nothing. Only then did it occur to me that if we said anything, the sound would travel to the hotel room from my phone to his—at least I assumed it worked that way. I should have studied the app more thoroughly.

"Look for the mute button," Jaxson coaxed.

We both tried to find it, but we failed. "We'll have to keep quiet," I said, and everyone nodded that they understood.

I swear it was at least fifteen minutes before I heard a knock on the motel door. Uh-oh. If Morgana was tied up, who would open it? Mauricio was a smart man. If he cared for Morgana—or needed to kill her—he'd figure a way in.

"Sandra?" That was Mauricio. Steve must have left the door unlocked. Good thinking on his part, but it might clue Mauricio into the fact that this was another trap.

"Mmm…mmmm." Steve must have gagged her.

I couldn't see all that much since the camera phone was pointed away from her.

Footsteps sounded. Part of Mauricio's image appeared. He leaned over and removed her gag.

"Morgana! Where's Sandra?" he asked.

"Thank goodness you came. She left. All she said was that she'd be back. Sandra must be looking for someone." Her words came out rushed and sounded very sincere to me.

"Tell me what happened. When she called me, she was talking nonsense about wanting to kill you."

Nonsense? Did Mauricio assume this was another set-up and he wasn't going to say anything or was he telling the truth? I looked over at Jaxson. This wasn't how I thought this conversation would go down.

"I know my sister hates me for taking Daniel away from her, even though they'd broken up. Now she thinks you and I will get back together, and that is unacceptable to her. Sandra wants you very much."

He shook his head. "I doubt that."

"It's true. I know she loves you."

I had to admit, Morgana continued to impress me with her acting skills.

"You're wrong," he said. "Come on. Let's get you out of here before Sandra returns. I'll deal with her later—once you're safe."

Surprisingly, Morgana didn't make some excuse as to why she needed to stay. When they left, I sagged against the seat. "This isn't good."

"No, it's not," Jaxson said.

"I really thought Mauricio would say Morgana had been a thorn in Sandra's side for too long, and that she was willing to pay a lot to have him kill Morgana. Mauricio would then wave his hands and say his spell. Only he'd fail."

"How would he know he failed?" Gavin asked. "Do we think the person suddenly turns a slight shade of gray and begins to cough?"

I hadn't thought about that. "No. I don't think your dad had any idea he'd been cursed until a few days went by."

"How are we going to know if his powers have been destroyed if we can't catch him in the act of doing a spell?" Gavin asked.

"We can't. So much for my brilliant plan. It definitely was a bust." I sat up straighter. "What about poor Morgana? I can't imagine she wants to be with Mauricio right now."

"I'll call Steve," Nash said. "He needs to stop them some-how."

"Good idea. Best case scenario is that Mauricio takes her

back to the hotel."

"Do you really think he wants Morgana blabbing to the cops about what went down?" Rihanna said.

"What could she say? Nothing happened. The only person who looks guilty is Sandra, and she wasn't even the one talking to Mauricio."

"I'm sure Steve understands the potential danger Morgana is in. He's not going to let any harm come to her," Nash said.

"I hope not."

A minute later, Elissa's phone rang. "Thank goodness. It's Chris calling me back."

It took a second for me to remember that was Dr. Chris Williams, the medical examiner in Miami. "Can you put him on speaker?"

"Sure." She swiped the icon. "Hey, Chris. Thanks for getting back to me."

"Sorry. I've been with my mom. She's been ill. I just now saw your message."

"Not to worry. I hope she's going to be okay."

"Thanks. She will be with rest. In regard to your inquiry about the black-heart deaths, I'm so glad you asked. It's been driving me crazy. About a week ago, we received a body whose heart had practically petrified."

"Did you figure out the cause of death?"

"No, but we're still looking. I'm assuming your medical examiner had the same issue?"

"Yes, only the heart belonged to my ex-husband."

Dr. Williams sucked in a breath. "That's terrible. I'm sorry."

"Thanks. The strange part is that he was seemingly

healthy a few days before."

"Same with this woman."

"Can you send me your findings, and I'll do the same to you?"

"Of course. As to your other query, Mauricio Jimenez volunteers here three times a week. He's an outstanding doctor who needs to complete some course work before he can be licensed to work in Florida. Why do you ask?"

Elissa looked up at us. Nash motioned for the phone. "This is deputy Nash Solano of the Witch's Cove sheriff's department. We're hoping he can help us with a murder investigation."

"Oh, sure. He called a little while ago and said he wouldn't be in for a few days, but I'll tell him you asked for his help."

"Thanks."

Elissa and her former work partner chatted a bit more, and then she hung up. "What do you think?" she asked.

"Mauricio could be involved in Daniel's death, but we can't be sure," Nash said. "Is it possible he tampered with the heart of the other dead person to make sure he wasn't implicated?"

She shook her head. "That would only make things worse. Chris would take a picture of the heart the moment he removed the organ. He'd know immediately if something strange happened. There's nothing Mauricio could have done to change that."

The sheriff department's front door opened, and Steve came in with Hunter, Misty, and Morgana. I jumped up, happy to see she was safe. Instead of Morgana coming into the conference room, he escorted her into his office.

Nash pushed back his chair. "Let me see what that is all about."

I was glad to see he thought it strange, too. I wondered where Mauricio was, and why was Steve trying to hide Morgana? Did Steve think Mauricio would barge into the office and demand to see her?

Until Steve returned, I had no hope of getting answers to all of my questions.

Jaxson reached up. "Sit down, Glinda. Steve seems to have everything under control."

I sat. "I'm glad that Morgana is safe, as is everyone else, but Mauricio is a big unknown."

"When I get the report from Chris about the other body, if the two have identical symptoms, we'll conclude that the issue started in Miami," Elissa said.

"Even if we find out that Mauricio put a curse on Daniel and this other person, do you really think he acted alone?"

No one said anything for a moment. Finally, Elissa shook her head. "No, I don't. Admittedly, he knew Daniel since Mauricio worked for Morgana, but by then, he and Morgana were history. If anything, he should have killed Morgana, not Daniel."

That's what I'd always thought. "Then who had it out for Gavin's dad?" I asked.

She looked over at her son. "What do you think? Daniel and I didn't really communicate much."

"If I had to point a finger at anyone, I'd say Sandra had the most motive to want him gone."

"In order to be partner in the law firm?" I asked. "Murder

is a bit extreme."

Gavin shrugged. "True, but he wasn't really nice to her in the last year, mostly because Morgana had a grudge against her sister, and Dad wanted to be supportive. At least that is what he told me."

"Did your dad tell you about the grudge or feud?" I asked.

"A little. Mostly it was that Morgana was jealous of her sister, because Sandra was the successful one. I don't know Morgana all that well, but Dad would drop little hints about their many family feuds. Sandra worked hard while Morgana relied on her looks to get what she wanted."

"That would make Sandra jealous of Morgana."

"Maybe, but all I can say for sure is that the two sisters didn't see eye-to-eye."

"It would make sense then if Sandra had been the one to pull the puppet strings," Jaxson said. "But do we have any proof she's connected to Daniel's death or Elissa's kidnapping?"

I don't know why he asked. Jaxson knew it was all supposition. "No, but it sounds logical."

Nash and Steve returned to the conference room, which meant Misty and Hunter must be staying with Morgana.

Nash sat while Steve remained standing. "I'm sure you all have questions. I, too, heard what was going on with Mauricio and Morgana. And no, it didn't go down as I'd thought either. When the two left together, I wasn't sure what Mauricio's plan was regarding Morgana. While it appeared as if he was driving her back to the hotel, I decided to intervene. I pulled them over on the premise that some salesperson had reported Morgana had shoplifted."

"I bet that surprised her," Gavin said, sounding quite delighted.

"Naturally, she defended herself, but she's a smart woman. Eventually, she realized that she'd be safer with me than with Mauricio. She told him not to worry about her, that it was all a misunderstanding. She said she'd meet him back in Miami in a few days."

"He bought it?" Mauricio seemed smarter than that. "I'm surprised he didn't think it odd that you could recognize a tourist driving in someone else's car."

"You're right. I would be suspicious, but for whatever reason, he didn't say anything. He might have been trying to come up with a reason why he was with Morgana. I don't know. From what he told me, he plans to spend the night at the hotel and then drive back tomorrow morning. I've asked Misty if she could supply a few undercover cops to make sure he doesn't pull a fast one."

"That's smart. I, for one, will feel better once he returns to Miami. I just wish I knew if he was *defused*, so to speak," I said.

Steve nodded. "Don't we all. I'm thankful that Elissa is back and that no one else was hurt."

"You're right. We should be thankful for what we have."

It was just that loose ends weren't my thing.

Chapter Eighteen

J AXSON AND I were at the Tiki Hut Grill at lunch a few days later when he pressed on my hand. "Is there any way you can stop that tapping?"

I looked up at him. "What are you talking about?"

He nodded to the spoon. "You've been banging that thing on the table for the last thirty seconds. Something must be on your mind."

"There is. Even though Mauricio left three days ago, and Morgana left yesterday with her husband's ashes, I feel unsettled."

"I get it. Everything seems as if things are back to normal, and yet we've had no closure to either who was behind Elissa's capture or who killed Daniel."

"I know who killed Daniel. We just can't prove it was Mauricio or if he acted alone."

Jaxson let go of my hand. "You know the old saying: you can't win 'em all."

"I know, but it's still frustrating. I keep coming back to the message on the mirror."

"That your grandmother's necklace told you the truth."

"Yes, but there has to be something I'm missing."

Just then Steve came into the restaurant. He nodded to us

and said something to Aunt Fern. They chatted for a bit before he stopped over to our table.

"I have some news I thought you'd like to hear."

My slight depression immediately evaporated. "Pull up a chair."

Steve sat. "I received a call from Detective Bogart."

"He's the man who was working Daniel's case from Miami, right?"

"Yes. He found the two men who kidnapped Elissa."

"That's great news."

"As we expected, they were just some thugs for hire. After threatening them with a lot of jail time, they gave up the name of the person who hired them."

"It was Sandra, wasn't it? I knew it," I said with a smile.

"Actually, it wasn't."

I sat up straighter. "Then who?"

"Ed Whitlow."

"Seriously? Why? I mean, I knew he was suing Daniel Sanchez because he believed the lawyer botched the case against his ex-wife, but what does that have to do with Elissa?"

"The detective interviewed Whitlow, but of course, he denied everything. I have to say, with the amount of money this guy has, it will be hard to catch him. He's got shell corporations and lots of ways to keep his distance from anything dirty."

"Does that mean the detective let him go?" Of course, he did. The word of two felons wouldn't hold much weight without any proof.

"For the moment, yes. I thought you should know."

Aunt Fern carried over a To-Go cup of coffee for the

sheriff. Most likely, he asked for the drink as an excuse to see if we were here.

"Thanks for letting us know."

"You bet."

Once Steve left, I didn't feel much better. "If we believe the two hired hands, then one mystery is solved, even though there is no satisfaction in that."

"Because we didn't solve the crime?"

"That and I want to learn more about Mauricio." I held up a hand. "And don't you dare say that something will come up."

Jaxson laughed. "It always does. Speaking of things coming up, have you decided if you are going to your tenth high school reunion? I saw the invitation on the desk."

We had been talking about going. And by *we*, I meant Jaxson's brother and I, since we graduated together. Until Jaxson came into my life, Drake and I had been fairly inseparable. His wine and cheese shop started to thrive just when our Witch's Cove deputy was murdered, and Jaxson became the main suspect.

"I'm leaning toward saying yes. This case seems to be over, so it might be fun to see everyone again."

"What percent would you say might come?"

"Maybe fifty percent of the class. I know a lot moved out of town, and I'm not sure if they'd want to return."

"January is often the coldest month. We might be chilly at times, but we're a lot warmer than most places."

"Good point." I finished off my coffee and was ready to head back to the office, even though we didn't have much to do.

Before I could push back my chair, Rihanna and Gavin came in. The moment they saw us, they headed over. "We have news."

My first thought was a scary one. They were eighteen and nineteen, and I feared they'd announce they were engaged or something crazy like that.

"Tell me."

They pulled up a chair. "Mom got the autopsy report back from Dr. Williams regarding the other black-heart."

That wasn't our case, but maybe it would point a finger at Mauricio. How though, I don't know. "And?"

"You'll never guess who it belonged to." Gavin smiled.

"I don't know anyone in Miami. Tell me."

"Ed Whitlow's ex-wife."

I was stunned. "The same woman Ed was trying to prevent from getting all of his alimony?"

"The one and the same," Gavin said.

"Wow. I bet Detective Bogart will be questioned Ed Whitlow again." I looked over at Jaxson. "If those two ex-cons are to be believed, Mr. Whitlow hired them two thugs to kidnap Elissa, but then for some reason, they walked out and left her alone in the warehouse. Did we ever hear why they did that?" I wonder if it had anything to do with his ex-wife's death.

"No, but let's hope Detective Bogart can get them to talk. Ed won't be admitting to anything."

"Where does that leave us?" I asked.

"The Miami police need to find proof that Whitlow was involved, and the word of two felons probably doesn't count for much," Gavin said.

"We have a better chance of it snowing here tomorrow."

"Have some faith, Glinda."

"I'm trying, and yes, I know something might come up."

BECAUSE I'D BEEN in a funk ever since Daniel Sanchez's murder case turned cold, I decided to accept the invitation to our high school reunion. Maybe seeing some old friends would do me good. I was just about to call Drake and tell him I'd be his date since Jaxson said I'd have a better time with his brother when a knock sounded on our office door.

Usually, most people just came in. As I stood to answer it, Steve popped his head in and looked around. "Are Rihanna and Jaxson here?"

He sounded serious. "Jaxson is downstairs, and Rihanna is in her bedroom. Want me to get them?" Of course, he did, or he wouldn't have asked about them.

"Please."

I texted Jaxson and then went to Rihanna's bedroom. "Steve is here for some reason. I imagine he wants to tell us something. Can you spare the time to chat?" She seemed to be in the middle of a school project.

"Sure."

By the time Rihanna put away what she was working on, Jaxson had come up the back staircase. He looked at Steve and then at me. I just shrugged.

"Have a seat," Steve said.

"What happened?" I wasn't up for more bad news.

"Mauricio Jimenez is dead."

Well, stun me with a taser. "Dead? How can that be?" The three of us sat there without saying a word for a moment. Finally, I had to ask the question that everyone had to be thinking. "How did he die?"

"Now that is the interesting part. The autopsy is not complete, but on first glance, his heart had turned black and hard."

I froze. "That means there is another warlock out there. I can't believe it. I was positive Mauricio was our warlock who killed Daniel."

"Looks like he might not have been. The police believe Mauricio died in almost the same manner as Gavin's dad, which means Mauricio didn't kill Daniel."

Oh, no. Levy and his coven thought they'd stripped his powers to prevent him from turning other hearts black, but it was all for naught. "Who do they think is responsible?"

"That's where it gets interesting. They checked Mauricio's cabana and found his phone. When they searched his cell records, guess who had left him messages several times before Daniel died and again when Mauricio returned from Witch's Cove?"

"Who?"

"Ed Whitlow."

"Him again?"

Jaxson shook his head. "The man's wife was killed by a warlock. Is it possible he hired Mauricio to kill her and not Daniel Sanchez?" He waved a hand. "That makes no sense. Another warlock had to have entered the picture and killed Mauricio. Or maybe it was a witch who has these extraordinary powers."

"The cops are going through Ed's correspondences now to see if he shut up Mauricio, but at the moment, the connection between them is still uncertain."

This was mind boggling. "It kind of implies Ed Whitlow is a warlock. It's not like Mauricio's own powers killed him."

"Why not kill his wife himself?" Jaxson asked.

"He didn't want to be connected to her death. I don't know. The puzzle pieces are not fitting."

"I agree. Just so you know, I asked Elissa to assist in the autopsy to make sure we weren't missing anything. She'll be doing it virtually, of course. I didn't want her anywhere near Miami."

Rihanna let out a breath. "I know Gavin would say thank you."

"Now what?" I asked.

"Now we wait," Steve said.

That was my least favorite thing to do. Steve left with the promise he'd let us know the moment he learned anything.

Once he was gone, I turned to Jaxson. "I guess you're going to say this is exactly what you figured would happen."

"How could I have anticipated Mauricio would die?"

"No, I mean that something turned up. Only now we have more clues than we want."

He smiled. "You are never happy, pink lady. Too many clues or too few. I should call you Pinkilocks."

"That's funny." I turned to Rihanna. "What do you think about trying to contact Nana?"

"Why?"

"We need answers, and I have the sense Nana can help."

Rihanna shrugged. "Remember, I kind of failed last time I

tried."

"I don't think you failed. Nana could have been the one to find Elissa and help guide her back to the station."

"I think Elissa found her own way to town," Rihanna said.

"Maybe, but even you have to agree that the message on the mirror had to have been from her, especially since she signed it with an N."

"You're probably right," Rihanna said.

Jaxson wrapped his arms around me and pulled me closer. "You need to relax or all that anxiety will damage your mind."

That was hard to do. "I could if I knew why Mauricio died and who was behind Daniel's death."

Jaxson leaned back. "You don't ask for much, do you?"

I smiled. "No. I want what I want." I tapped his chest. "And that includes you."

He clasped my hand and pressed my fingers against his lips. "That's so nice to hear."

I'd basically told him I loved him only a short while ago, but I wasn't in the right frame of mind to bring that up at the moment—or think about it. Rihanna was here, and she might read my mind, which would be a bit embarrassing.

Just then Iggy crawled out from under the sofa. "Knock it off you two. All this sweet talk is making me sick."

We all laughed. "What's your take, Iggy, on Mauricio's death?"

"What if this Ed guy isn't a warlock, but rather Mauricio had used this time-stopping powder spell stuff before?"

Only then did I recall what Mauricio said when the powder came at him. "Jaxson, how would you describe Mauricio's reaction to the potion I threw at him?"

"His reaction? Confusion at first and then total and utter fear."

I lifted up Iggy and kissed him.

"Hey, what was that for?" He dragged his claw over his face as if he was trying to erase the kiss.

"For solving the case."

"Me? What did I do? I've been stuck in your purse for the better part of a week. Ever since coming back here, I've barely left the office."

"Then for being super smart."

He lifted one leg. "Well, I am that."

"What nugget of knowledge did Iggy just give you?" Jaxson asked.

"Remember I told you that I could only use the time-stopping potion one time?"

"Yes, and if you used it a second time, or if someone used it against you, it could possibly harm you—if you were evil."

I waited for him to draw the same conclusion I had, but Jaxson looked at me blank-faced. "Yes. What if Mauricio had been involved with this time-freezing potion before? If this was his second contact, the potion might have taken his evil abilities and used it against him. The reaction would be different for each sorcerer, because their powers would be different. For Mauricio, he used spells to turn hearts black. This powder somehow knew that and turned his heart black."

A second later, Jaxson's eyes widened and he whistled. "Iggy's right." He laughed. "That is fantastic."

How had I not connected the dots before? As if Nana was in the room, my pendant flashed pink for a few seconds.

Rihanna sat up straighter. "Was that Nana saying she agreed?"

I grinned. "I think so." I clasped my hand around the pendant and found it warm to the touch. While I had no proof, I was pretty sure she was here with us just now.

"Thank you, Nana."

Once more the pendant flashed, and my heart warmed. We'd more or less solved the case—or at least the part of who—or rather what—killed Mauricio.

Chapter Nineteen

One week later

STEVE CALLED AND asked if Jaxson, Rihanna, and I would join him in his office. From the fact he sounded happy, I had the sense he might have more news about the case, even though I was convinced we'd solved most of it.

"I'm coming with you," Iggy announced. "After all, I figured out who killed Mauricio."

"Yes, you did. Mauricio's own evil killed him. You can come but keep a low profile. This is Steve's show."

"I always keep quiet."

I ran a gaze down his body. "Are you Iggy Goodall, or did someone switch you out with a mellower version of my familiar?"

"Funny, funny." He spun around and crawled into my big bag.

As much as I wanted to speculate what this could mean, I thought it best to wait and see what Steve had to say. When we arrived, Nash, Elissa, and Gavin were already in the conference room.

After grabbing a much-needed cookie from Pearl, we headed on in.

"Good, you are all here," Steve said.

"Did you learn something?" I asked, even though the

answer was obviously yes.

"I did. Have a seat."

Rihanna sat next to Gavin, and we sat on the other side of Steve. "Tell us. The suspense is killing me."

Steve smiled. "I'll let Elissa go first."

"As you know, I helped with the virtual autopsy. It was my first one. What struck me about Mauricio's heart was that it was covered in a brown substance."

I pumped a fist. "I knew it. Or rather Iggy kind of figured it out first."

"What do you mean?" she asked.

I explained about the restrictions of this potion. "If Mauricio had used this potion before to incapacitate his victim, for example, then when I used it on him, it turned his own spells against him."

"Which meant it turned Mauricio's heart to stone?" Elissa asked.

"Yes. Did you test to see what that powder was?"

"I did, or rather I asked the Miami lab to do an analysis of it, but they are stumped. Do you think I could get a small sample and send it to their lab?"

Since she wasn't a witch, I saw no reason why not. "I bought it at the Hex and Bones Apothecary. Bertha's granddaughter sold it to me, but ask Bertha. She knows all about it."

Elissa smiled. "I will, but no lab tech or ME will understand or believe magic was involved."

"True, but they can tell you if the powders match. Even if they say the cause of both deaths are undetermined, we'll know."

"Yes, we will."

Elissa nodded to Steve to indicate she was done. "Okay, folks. For the big news. Between the texts found on Mauricio's phone and some money sent to Mauricio, we know that Ed Whitlow hired Mauricio to kill his wife."

That really came as no surprise. "Because he was too cheap to pay alimony?"

"The detective didn't say, but it's possible he wanted to make his ex-wife miserable. When the judge ruled in her favor, Ed had to do something."

"Wow. That was one unhappy man," I said.

"No kidding," Nash said.

"Was Ed involved in my Dad's death, too?" Gavin asked.

"Actually, no. For a slightly reduced sentence, Ed told us where he learned about Mauricio and his special powers."

"Sandra?" I blurted.

"Bingo."

I had to say, I felt pretty good for having guessed it all along. "Why did he say she wanted Daniel dead?"

"She wanted to be partner in their law firm."

"Dad would have given the position up in a heartbeat to stay alive."

"I'm sorry, Gavin. Greed makes people do strange things."

"Can the Miami PD prove what Ed Whitlow said is true?"

"They are working on it now. I believe they are getting a warrant to search her bank records, phone records, etc."

"Regardless of what they find, my gut says she's guilty," I threw in.

As if my necklace had a mind of its own, it flashed pink, and everyone stilled.

"What was that?" Steve asked.

"It's never done that until this case. I think Nana is communicating with me."

"If she's a reliable source, perhaps we should hire her."

The group laughed.

"Any idea who had Elissa kidnapped?" I asked. I really didn't like loose ends.

"Ed finally admitted to that crime. He hired the two thugs. Because Sandra helped set up Daniel to take the fall for falsifying the papers in regard to Ed's divorce, he owed her. Sandra was the one who asked him to handle Elissa's kidnapping."

"Why?" Jaxson asked.

"Because you were getting suspicious about Mauricio, she wanted the four of you out of Miami ASAP. What better way than to put Gavin's mom in danger. The plan was never to hurt Elissa."

"Wow. Is that enough to arrest her?" My knowledge of the law was limited.

"If they can confirm what Ed said is true, then yes. Whether she hired Mauricio to kill Daniel is another matter. If she is guilty, I have faith the good men in Miami will find proof. It's just a matter of time."

"Good enough for me." And I meant it. Everything pointed to Sandra being involved in Daniel's death.

"If she conspired to have Elissa kidnapped, she'll be thrown in jail and then disbarred. If they can prove she hired Mauricio to kill Daniel, she'd go away for a very long time."

"Do you think we'll get confirmation that Sandra paid Mauricio to kill Daniel?" I asked Jaxson later that night.

"Does it really matter?" Jaxson asked.

His back was to me since he was kneeling down in front of his fireplace stoking the flames. I sighed. Being here with him made all of the questions about the case almost disappear.

"I don't think she should be allowed to go free if she is guilty."

He stood and returned to the sofa. "I couldn't agree more."

I handed him the bowl of popcorn. Solving cases took a lot out of us, but I wouldn't choose another career.

We'd rented a movie that I was excited to watch. Of course, it was a murder mystery.

Just as he was about to turn on the television, my cell rang. I wasn't going to answer it since that would be rude.

"Aren't you going to take that? You know you want to."

In case it was Rihanna or my mom, I picked up my phone.

"Hey, it's Steve," he said.

My pulse soared. "Can I put you on speaker? I'm with Jaxson."

"Of course."

"Go ahead."

"The Miami boys are fast workers. They found the money trail that connects Sandra to Mauricio. It was done using some privacy cryptocurrency coin, but they were still able to figure out who sent it and where it went."

"That's fantastic. Is that enough to arrest her?"

"It might not have been until the men in blue received a

note from Mauricio."

I looked over at Jaxson who didn't seem to understand either. "What did it say?"

"It was one of those *in-case-of-my-death* notes. He'd given the note to a friend who had no idea what was in the envelope. It basically outlined everything he and Sandra agreed upon."

"Did it mention his magical ability to kill?" I asked.

"Not specifically, but it's enough to put Sandra in jail for a long time."

"That's great news. Thank you."

"You bet. And thank you guys, too. I'm not sure we could have done it without all of you."

Heat raced up my face. "Thanks for being open-minded about my magic."

"You bet."

Steve hung up, and I turned to Jaxson. "Is that not amazing?"

He looked unaffected. "As I always said, something was bound to come up."

I laughed. "And it did. I think this calls for a celebration."

"What do you have in mind?"

I did what I've been wanting to do for a long time. I wrapped my arms around his neck and kissed him. I was right where I wanted to be and had no intention of moving any time soon.

I hope you enjoyed the magical mystery of the pendant. I always love it when Nana helps out—even if she is from the other side. I personally am convinced our dearly departed are always with us. We just need to look for clues.

What's next? Glinda and Drake's tenth-year high school reunion, of course! And what's a reunion without a death? Glinda drags Drake into the fold of solving this mystery since it was his good high school buddy who's been killed. Sniff, sniff.

Buy on Amazon or read for FREE on Kindle Unlimited

Don't forget to sign up for my Cozy Mystery newsletter *to learn about my discounts and upcoming releases. If you prefer to only receive notices regarding my releases, follow me on BookBub.*
http://smarturl.it/VellaDayNL
bookbub.com/authors/vella-day

Here is a sneak peak of The Poisoned Pink Punch

DRAKE HARRISON KNOCKED on my bedroom door. "You've been in there a long time, Glinda."

Both Jaxson Harrison, my partner in the Pink Iguana Sleuths' Agency, and his brother, Drake, were waiting in my living room, but only Drake and I were going to our tenth high school reunion. Jaxson's tenth reunion had been six years ago.

"I'm almost ready." I checked my image in the mirror once more. I'd already changed my outfit three times. Enough was enough. Impressing others might have been my MO in high school, but no longer. I was a respected business owner now. It didn't matter—or at least it shouldn't matter—what my old high school friends thought of me.

Inhaling, I pushed open the door, lifted my arms in the air, and twirled around. "Tada!"

Jaxson whistled. "Maybe I should come with you guys so I can fend off the men."

I laughed, though I adored him for thinking I looked good. "You don't think everyone will be disappointed that I'm not dressed all in pink?"

"What are you talking about? You have on a pink blouse and pink earrings."

I plucked the black skirt from my legs. "Hel-lo!"

Drake rolled his eyes at his brother. "I'm glad you have to deal with her every day."

"Now you're just being mean. Admittedly, I usually only wear my pink signature color, but I can handle some variety now and again."

Iggy, my pink iguana familiar, poked his head out from under the sofa. "Can I come with you?"

"To the reunion? Why?"

"Where you go, disaster often follows," he said.

"That is not true—at least not all of the time." I looked over at Jaxson for some help.

He stepped over to Iggy and picked him up. "I thought you wanted to spend the evening with me, buddy. We were going to watch some TV."

"I guess that would be okay. Can I ask Aimee to come over?" Aimee was my aunt's cat who lived across the hallway from us. Aimee, like Iggy, could talk.

"Sure." He placed Iggy on the sofa, and then Jaxson hugged me. "Have a good time, but watch out for Drake. He can be unruly at times."

I chuckled. That was the farthest thing from the truth. Jaxson had always been the troubled older brother. "Don't worry. I'll make sure he doesn't step out of line."

Drake touched my arm. "Come on. We're already late."

Who wanted to be the first to arrive at a party anyway? Oh, yeah. Drake did. I stood on my tiptoes and kissed Jaxson goodbye. "You don't have to babysit the animal, you know."

He grinned. "I know."

"Who are you calling an animal?" Iggy huffed.

"Behave for Jaxson." I wagged a finger at him, though I had no doubt the two of them would have a good time—or at least Iggy would. He adored my boyfriend.

After Iggy assured me he'd behave, Drake and I headed downstairs. Being the gentleman that he was, Drake insisted he chauffeur me the three miles to the high school.

Rihanna, my eighteen-year old cousin, had volunteered to head the party's decoration committee. She, along with her two new girlfriends, Casi and Lena, promised to make it an evening to remember. I hoped that meant the theme would include some pink.

Drake glanced over at me. "Are you nervous?"

I knew why he asked. I often obsessed over things. "Surprisingly, no. I have a successful business, a boyfriend, and a drop-dead gorgeous escort for the night." I'd heard that being unattached at one of these reunions was a big no-no. Or at least for women it seemed to be.

He chuckled. "Thanks. I don't say it often enough, but

I'm proud of all you've accomplished since high school."

"Aw, thank you, but look at you. You've done ever better."

"Maybe, but it has come at a cost. I've been so consumed making my cheese and wine shop a success that I've barely had time to date. Not to mention, I've miss our little talks," he said.

"Me, too, but we can blame that on Jaxson." His brother had been helping Drake with inventory and such until Jaxson and I teamed up to open our sleuth agency, which meant Drake had to pick up the slack. Thankfully, he'd recently found more part-time help.

Drake laughed. "Let's do that. As his penance, my brother needs to give you up at least twice a month so the two of us can create our ice cream sundae masterpieces."

"I love doing that with you." I twisted toward him. "How did a health nut end up being your brother?"

He shook his head. "Some mysteries will never be solved."

Before we could decide how the two brothers could be so different, we arrived at the school parking lot. The flashing sheriff's car lights shot my senses to high alert. "What are Steve and Nash doing here? I can't imagine our class is that rowdy."

Drake parked. "Let's see what's going on."

When he reached the double doors that led into the gym, Nash Solano, our deputy, blocked our way. "Glinda. Drake. I'm afraid there's been an incident. Steve asked I keep out all new arrivals."

"What kind of incident are we talking about?" I was fairly confident that we could talk our way inside. I'd saved Nash's life recently, and he owed us.

"Someone died."

I sucked in a body-trembling breath. "Who was it?"

He checked his notepad. "A Kyle Covington."

Drake grabbed my arm. "Kyle? You have to be kidding."

"I take it you knew him?" Nash asked.

"Yes. We were on the debate and wrestling team together and were good friends."

Nash looked over at me. "Since I know Glinda will worm her way into this investigation at some point, I'll let you guys through, but don't touch anything—especially you, Glinda. If you spot anyone who might have a motive for wanting this man dead, please let us know."

I might have been offended that he thought I'd *worm* my way into an investigation, but since this was a friend of Drake's, I had to help, and Nash knew that. "I guess this means he was murdered?"

"I spoke too soon. I've been assigned door duty, that's all, but Steve might have more information."

That was a line if ever I'd ever heard one, but we'd find out the truth soon enough. As we entered the gym that had a rather festive blue and black decor with a splash of pink thrown in for good measure, I couldn't help but experience a trickle of excitement. It was totally uncalled for and inappropriate at a time like this, but it was a bit thrilling to be asked to help with a murder for a change—assuming Kyle had been killed.

A surprising number of people were there, which suggested Steve had asked all those present to stay around so he could question them. Even if the sheriff didn't know for sure Kyle had been killed, he might have wanted to cover his bases in case it turned out to be the case.

I spotted my cousin Rihanna off to the side, huddled with her two new girlfriends, and we headed toward them.

Hopefully, one of them saw what happened. For sure, Steve wouldn't share what he'd learned—at least not until the medical examiner gave him her report.

"Rihanna, what is going on?" I asked.

"Glinda. I'm so glad you're here. I don't know much other than Casi and Lena had just delivered the punch bowl to the main table when someone started screaming that a man had collapsed."

"Did either of you girls see anything?"

Lena shook her head, and Casi ran her palms down her skirt. "Sort of. After I heard the punchbowl crash to the ground, I turned around and saw some guy lying there. I think he died like right away," Casi reported. "But I didn't see anyone near him or anything."

"How terrible for you to witness that."

She nodded. Since my parents owned the funeral home in town, I was used to dead bodies, but this girl didn't seem to be.

Drake touched my arm. "I'm going over there to make sure it really is Kyle."

"Sure." I understood his need to be certain there hadn't been a mistake. I'd never had a friend my age die, and I couldn't imagine what that would be like. I turned back to the girls. "Did the sheriff say everyone had to remain in the gym until he'd questioned them?" That's what he'd done at our Halloween party when my Aunt Fern's boyfriend had been killed.

"Yes," Lena said.

Just then our medical examiner and her son—who happened to be Rihanna's boyfriend—arrived. I expected my cousin to dart over to him, but she remained where she was. Gavin must have told her that when he was working a crime scene that she needed to stay back.

"Did you know the dead guy, too?" Casi asked.

"A little. I mean, Drake and I were the ones who were close. Only because he and Kyle were good friends did we talk sometimes." I had to search my mind for when we'd interacted other than when I was with Drake. Ten years was a long time. "Kyle and I had a couple of math classes together, but he mostly kept to himself. Back then, I was trying to figure out how to fit in, and I wasn't looking for a boyfriend or anything. Even then, I could tell Kyle was destined to do great things. The guy was a genius."

Drake returned. From the vacant look in his eyes, it was not good news. "It's Kyle. I can't believe it."

I hugged him. "I'm sorry, Drake."

"Thanks." He shook his head. "I couldn't see any evidence of murder. It appears as if he drank the punch, had some kind of reaction—or maybe even a heart attack—and then knocked over the bowl as he collapsed. There's pink punch everywhere."

"Good thing time of death was known. Otherwise, the cold punch might have affected his core body temperature."

Drake dipped his chin. "Glinda."

Dang it. I was being too clinical and not a sympathetic friend. It was the way I often coped with tragedy. "Sorry. Did

Steve say anything?"

"What could he say other than he could tell I was upset? Mr. Vincent is taking names and asking questions."

I craned my neck and spotted our principal. "That's smart of Steve to ask him to take roll. Mr. Vincent might be old, but the man never forgets a student. If Steve had spoken to everyone, someone might have lied about their identity."

"If I'd put something in the punch," Lena said, "I wouldn't give my real name."

The punch being spiked with poison was a good theory, but only if Kyle had been the only one who drank from it. Because no one else appeared ill, it wasn't clear what had happened. "I'm sure many would do the same, but Mr. Vincent will spot the liars."

Drake clasped my arm. "As long as we're here, we should mingle."

Now it was my turn to dip my chin. "You want to catch up with old friends?" That wasn't like him.

"No. I want to see who's here. Kyle wasn't the most liked guy in the school if you recall."

I shrugged. "I think I was too into my pink clothing and my studies to have noticed." Not to mention my magic.

"Assuming he didn't die of a heart attack or some other natural cause, who are you thinking might have wanted him dead?" Rihanna asked.

My cousin would make a great sleuth one day. Okay, to be fair, she already was a pretty good one. Rihanna could not only read minds under certain circumstances, she could connect the dots when others often couldn't.

"His death could be from natural causes, but Kyle still

looked fit," Drake said. "To be honest, we lost touch a few years back after one of his online trading schemes hit it big."

"Trading, as in stock trading?" That was fascinating. With my math background, I probably would have done quite well in that field had I pursued it.

"Yes, but then he got into cryptocurrencies—Bitcoin, I think—along with a few Alt coins. He invested when those coins cost pennies. Then the price skyrocketed, and he became mega rich, or so I read."

"That might have upset a few people."

Drake looked around. "True, but none of those people would be at our ten-year high school reunion."

"I wouldn't be too sure. Jealousy can cut deep, and those kinds of people can be creative. Admittedly, holding a grudge for ten years seems remote," I said.

"I won't discount anything. Kyle won a lot of debate tournaments during his high school career. The last one allowed him to compete at States—which he won."

The memories rushed back. "If I recall, that resulted in him receiving a full ride to Harvard. I bet whoever came in second might be angry at that lost opportunity."

"I suppose," Drake said. "The second runner up was Ronnie Taggert who ended up at Florida State. I don't know how he faired after that."

"Where did Kyle end up after college?" I asked.

"Last I heard, he was working in Silicon Valley."

That was so far from my world, I couldn't even imagine living in the corporate fast lane. "Good for him. Did he ever marry?"

"Not that I was aware, but as I said, we lost touch a few

years back."

"I can subtly find out about his marital status," Rihanna said.

I loved her enthusiasm. "That's okay. We'll find it out sooner or later."

Suddenly, a tall, redhead made a beeline toward us, looking as if she was on a mission. The beautiful woman appeared familiar, but I couldn't place her.

When she reached us, she broke into a dazzling smile. "Drake Harrison, is that really you?"

My protective instincts shot up, even though he and I were just friends. Drake spun to face her. "Yes?"

At least that made two of us who didn't know her.

"It's me. Andorra Leyton."

Drake's mouth gaped open. He then dragged his gaze from her head to her toes and back again. Okay, clearly he was impressed. "Andi? I can't believe it's you. You've changed."

She chuckled. "I hope for the better. Braces and glasses weren't a real good look for me back then."

"Ah, yeah. Definitely for the better." Drake all but drooled.

Once they finished hugging, I should have said something, but I, too, was in shock over her transformation. Andorra and I had only briefly interacted in high school. She'd mentioned she had some witch talents, but it wasn't something I wanted to explore at the time. Being a seventeen-year-old math geek made me enough of an outsider. I didn't need people learning about my abilities—limited as they were.

If I remembered correctly, Andorra Leyton had a crush on Drake, but back then, he was too focused on his studies, participating on the wrestling team, and trying to beat Kyle Covington at debate to give her the time of day.

Andorra faced me. "Is that you, Glinda?"

Expect for maybe a few added pounds, I hadn't changed all that much—or so I thought. "It sure is."

Before I could decide if I was happy to see her or not, she hugged me, too. Okay, that was unexpected. Andorra leaned back. "You look amazing. And the black skirt suits you."

Maybe she wasn't so bad after all. She smiled and then turned back to Drake. "I'm so sorry about Kyle. Is it a shock or what?"

"It's horrible," he said. "I still haven't wrapped my head around it. Did you hear anything?"

"As a matter of fact, I did."

Her words perked me up. "What do you find out?"

Buy on Amazon or read for FREE on Kindle Unlimited

THE END

A WITCH'S COVE MYSTERY (Paranormal Cozy Mystery)
PINK Is The New Black (book 1)
A PINK Potion Gone Wrong (book 2)
The Mystery of the PINK Aura (book 3)
Box Set (books 1-3)
Sleuthing In The PINK (book 4)
Not in The PINK (book 5)
Gone in the PINK of an Eye (book 6)
Box Set (books 4-6)
The PINK Pumpkin Party (book 7)
Mistletoe with a PINK Bow (book 8)
The Magical PINK Pendant (book 9)
The Poisoned PINK Punch (book 10)
PINK Smoke and Mirrors (book 11)
Broomsticks and PINK Gumdrops (book 12)

SILVER LAKE SERIES (3 OF THEM)
(1). HIDDEN REALMS OF SILVER LAKE (Paranormal
Romance)
Awakened By Flames (book 1)
Seduced By Flames (book 2)
Kissed By Flames (book 3)
Destiny In Flames (book 4)
Box Set (books 1-4)
Passionate Flames (book 5)
Ignited By Flames (book 6)
Touched By Flames (book 7)
Box Set (books 5-7)
Bound By Flames (book 8)
Fueled By Flames (book 9)
Scorched By Flames (book 10)

(2). FOUR SISTERS OF FATE: HIDDEN REALMS OF SILVER LAKE (Paranormal Romance)

Poppy (book 1)

Primrose (book 2)

Acacia (book 3)

Magnolia (book 4)

Box Set (books 1-4)

Jace (book 5)

Tanner (book 6)

(3). WERES AND WITCHES OF SILVER LAKE (Paranormal Romance)

A Magical Shift (book 1)

Catching Her Bear (book 2)

Surge of Magic (book 3)

The Bear's Forbidden Wolf (book 4)

Her Reluctant Bear (book 5)

Freeing His Tiger (book 6)

Protecting His Wolf (book 7)

Waking His Bear (book 8)

Melting Her Wolf's Heart (book 9)

Her Wolf's Guarded Heart (book 10)

His Rogue Bear (book 11)

Box Set (books 1-4)

Box Set (books 5-8)

Reawakening Their Bears (book 12)

OTHER PARANORMAL SERIES

PACK WARS (Paranormal Romance)

Training Their Mate (book 1)

Claiming Their Mate (book 2)

Rescuing Their Virgin Mate (book 3)
Box Set (books 1-3)
Loving Their Vixen Mate (book 4)
Fighting For Their Mate (book 5)
Enticing Their Mate (book 6)
Box Set (books 1-4)
Complete Box Set (books 1-6)

HIDDEN HILLS SHIFTERS (Paranormal Romance)
An Unexpected Diversion (book 1)
Bare Instincts (book 2)
Shifting Destinies (book 3)
Embracing Fate (book 4)
Promises Unbroken (book 5)
Bare 'N Dirty (book 6)
Hidden Hills Shifters Complete Box Set (books 1-6)

CONTEMPORARY SERIES
MONTANA PROMISES (Full length contemporary
Romance)
Promises of Mercy (book 1)
Foundations For Three (book 2)
Montana Fire (book 3)
Montana Promises Box Set (books 1-3)
Hart To Hart (Book 4)
Burning Seduction (Book 5)
Montana Promises Complete Box Set (books 1-5)

ROCK HARD, MONTANA (contemporary romance
novellas)
Montana Desire (book 1)
Awakening Passions (book 2)

PLEDGED TO PROTECT (contemporary romantic suspense)
From Panic To Passion (book 1)
From Danger To Desire (book 2)
From Terror To Temptation (book 3)
Pledged To Protect Box Set (books 1-3)

BURIED SERIES (contemporary romantic suspense)
Buried Alive (book 1)
Buried Secrets (book 2)
Buried Deep (book 3)
The Buried Series Complete Box Set (books 1-3)

A NASH MYSTERY (Contemporary Romance)
Sidearms and Silk(book 1)
Black Ops and Lingerie(book 2)
A Nash Mystery Box Set (books 1-2)

STARTER SETS (Romance)
Contemporary
Paranormal

Author Bio

Love it HOT and STEAMY? Sign up for my newsletter and receive MONTANA DESIRE for FREE. smarturl.it/o4cz93?IQid=MLite

OR Are you a fan of quirky PARANORMAL COZY MYSTERIES? Sign up for this newsletter. smarturl.it/CozyNL

Not only do I love to read, write, and dream, I'm an extrovert. I enjoy being around people and am always trying to understand what makes them tick. Not only must my romance books have a happily ever after, I need characters I can relate to. My men are wonderful, dynamic, smart, strong, and the best lovers in the world (of course).

My Paranormal Cozy Mysteries are where I let my imagination run wild with witches and a talking pink iguana who believes he's a real sleuth.

I believe I am the luckiest woman. I do what I love and I have a wonderful, supportive husband, who happens to be hot!

Fun facts about me

(1) I'm a math nerd who loves spreadsheets. Give me numbers and I'll find a pattern.

(2) I live on a Costa Rica beach!

(3) I also like to exercise. Yes, I know I'm odd.

I love hearing from readers either on FB or via email (hint, hint).

Social Media Sites

Website:
www.velladay.com

FB:
facebook.com/vella.day.90

Twitter:
@velladay4

Gmail:
velladayauthor@gmail.com

Printed in Great Britain
by Amazon